Thirsty

An Urban Novella by

La'Tonya West

Chapter One

Kaliyah drove up to the gas pump of the Exxon station blasting her favorite song, Sponsor by Tierra Marie. That song she felt described her to the teeth since she always had one or several men that took care of her. Of course in return she "took care" of them as well. Her mom, a crackhead and prostitute named Nettie, had told her at a very young age that as long as she had a pussy between her legs she should never be broke. That had proven to be the best piece of advice that Nettie ever gave her. Unlike her mother Kaliyah never did any drugs and the men that she laid with all had to be very wealthy. If their paper wasn't long they didn't stand a chance of getting a whiff of her sweet nookie! She really didn't care for black men too much but if their money was right she'd go ahead and make it do what it do. White men to her were a lot easier to deal with. They were a little more giving when it came to money. It seemed to take much more effort to get what she wanted from the brothers but none the less all men seemed to fall victim to her 5ft 9in. frame, caramel skin, grey eyes, perfect smile, perky 32B tits, thick thighs and round booty. She resembled the actress Stacey Dash and each time that someone told her that it made her head even bigger than what it already was. She was drop dead gorgeous and she knew it. In her words, she was a bad bitch! That's why she felt like she should be compensated for her services. She wasn't an average bitch so she refused to be treated like one. She'd always felt like she deserved only the best and so far she'd always had just that!

Today Kaliyah was pushin' her pink 2011 Chevy Corvette Zr1 that her sponsor Kent had given her for her birthday two months ago. He was a successful lawyer for a law firm by the name of Troutman & Saunders in Atlanta. Most of his clients were big named celebrities so he was very well paid. The two of them had met over a year ago at a charity event that she'd attended with one of her other sponsors, Greg, who was a doctor. Kent was there with his wife but throughout the entire evening his eyes were glued to her every move. Every move that she made she could feel his eyes on her.

The opportunity for her to slip him her number presented itself when she saw him excuse himself and head in the direction of the restrooms. She excused herself also, telling Greg that she needed to go to the ladies room. She took her time walking to the restroom hoping to catch him on his way out of the men's room. Her plan worked like a charm because as soon as she turned the corner he was coming out of the restroom. She walked up to him, handed him the torn piece of paper that she'd managed to scribble her number down on while Greg was mingling with his high-class friends. When she handed Kent the piece of paper he didn't ask any questions. He just slipped it inside his pocket and kept it moving. She'd done the same, going into the bathroom, washing her hands and making sure that she was still looking magnificent before going back out and joining Greg.

Kent hadn't wasted any time giving her a call. He called the very next day and asked her to meet him at the Marriot Hotel downtown. She made it clear to him over the phone that her "time" wasn't free and neither was it cheap. He informed her that money was no object for him and that was all she needed to hear. He turned out to be an undercover freak that secretly loved black women. She made sure that whenever he called for some of her good nookie she put it on him extremely good leaving him wanting more. In return he showered her with expensive gifts and money. The only problem that she had with him was the fact that he wanted her all to himself after they'd been messing around for a while. So she had to lie and pretend like she wasn't seeing anyone but him. She did whatever it took to keep him happy and to keep the money and the gifts flowing.

Back to the present day....

Kaliyah stepped out of her car, the mid-day sun kissing her caramel skin. She was wearing a strapless pink Chanel dress that stopped mid-thigh. On her feet she was wearing a pair of strappy pink Chanel sandals. The only jewelry that she wore was a necklace. The heart shaped charm that dangled from it was iced out. The long wavy dark brown laced front wig that she wore complimented her round face.

She swiped her credit card at the pump and then punched in her pin and the amount of gas that she wanted to purchase. Once her card had been approved she lifted the nozzle and placed it in the tank. She was leaning against her car singing along with Tierra Marie (the song was on repeat) and waiting for her tank to fill, when a black BMW with 24inch chrome rims pulled up behind her car. Lil' Wayne's voice was blaring from the speakers.

She rolled her eyes and sucked her teeth. "Lord please let my tank hurry up and finish filling. I don't have any time for some little wannabe thug to be all up in my face trying to holla at me." She said aloud.

The driver of the car opened up the door and stepped out. She saw him out of the corner of her eye. He was about 5'11, dark chocolate complexion, dreads that stopped just past his shoulders. He was wearing a white wifebeater and a pair of dark blue workman's Dickies. She could see that numerous tattoos decorated his arms. *Totally not my type!* She thought to herself. After he'd swiped his card he looked over at her and yelled over the music. "Hey lil mama, I'm Thrill, what's your name?"

Kaliyah put the nozzle back on the pump and shot him a disgusted look as she screwed her gas top back on. "My name is not interested." She yelled back over the music.

Thrill reached inside his car and turned down the music. "Excuse me, Miss Lady I didn't mean any harm." He chuckled. "I was just asking you your name. You are a very beautiful woman and I was hoping..."

Kaliyah held up her hand to stop him. "You were hoping nothing I don't waste my time on thugs or drug dealers! I like real men!"

Thrill looked at her as he wondered to himself who in the hell she thought she was talking to. She wasn't that damn fine. He licked his lips and ran his hand over his goat-tee. "That's good because I don't waste my time on stuck up fake bitches either!" He shot back. He didn't disrespect women on the regular but he felt that her snobby ass deserved to be put in her place! "And for the record I don't sell no motherfuckin' drugs! I get up every day and go to work!"

"Whatever! I guess that's why you're out here in the middle of the day riding around!" She rolled her eyes and proceeded to get into her car.

"It's called a lunch break you ignorant stuck up bitch! Don't you see these damn work pants I am wearing?" He yelled back! She had him heated. He couldn't stand bitches who tried to look down their noses at others like their shit didn't stink.

Kaliyah heard Thrill's last remark but instead of responding she got in her car and sped off. To her he was a nobody anyways so why waste her breath on him. Hell, his money wasn't long enough to deserve her attention. Thugs disgusted her to no end, she hated them! She couldn't for the life of her understand why most brothers chose that lifestyle. What really irked her nerves was how they walked around in clothes that were 10 sizes too big with their pants hanging off of their asses! Give her a man any day of the week rockin' a $3,000 Armani suit. Just thinking about it made her pussy juice up! Anything dealing with money did.

She got in her car and headed to meet up with her best friend Xavier for lunch. When she pulled up to Nan Thai Fine Dining, the valet opened up her door for her. He handed her a ticket and she slipped it inside of her pink Chanel bag and went inside of the restaurant. She told the hostess that she was there to meet a Mr. Young for lunch. The hostess showed her to the table where Xavier was seated and waiting for her. When he looked up and saw her headed in his direction, he stood to greet her. His blue eyes beamed as he extended his arms to give her a hug. He was as sweet as a cupcake but he was the best friend that anyone could ever ask for. He was 5'6, 115lbs, blue eyes, and blonde hair that was cut short and spiked. The two of them had been friends for more than five years now. They'd met where he worked, at Swan Coach House, which is an art gallery. She'd gone there with one of her sponsors. Xavier had been really nice and funny the whole time that they were there, telling them about the different pieces of art and cracking jokes. His sense of humor and knowledge about fashion had won her over, by the time that she and her date got ready to leave she had made a new friend and the two of them exchanged phone numbers.

When she reached the table she gave Xavier a hug and they took their seats. The hostess assured them that their waitress would be over shortly and left them to look over their menus. They both already knew what they wanted because this was their favorite restaurant and they came here often so they didn't need to look at the menu.

"Diva you are wearing that dress honey!" Xavier complimented her snapping his fingers as he eyed the Chanel dress that she was wearing. "Girl if we were the same size I would have to borrow that from you because I know it would look fabulous on my cute ass!"

"Thank you." Kaliyah replied not even cracking a smile.

Normally, if he gave her a compliment she'd be blushing and grinning from ear to ear. That told him that something was wrong. "What's the matter Diva? Which one of your men has worked your nerves now and do I need to break out my switchblade?" He said his voice resembling that of Wendy Williams.

She rubbed her temples as she felt a headache coming on. Thrill had really worked her nerves! She didn't appreciate him calling her out of her name. "No, you won't be needing your blade. I was at the gas station and some little wannabe thug was there also. The two of us exchanged words because he got upset with me for not being interested in him. He had the nerve to call me an ignorant bitch!"

Xavier's hand went up over his mouth like that was the most shocking thing that he'd ever heard in his life. He could be so overly dramatic at times, him and Kaliyah both, that's why the two of them got along so well because he was the male version of her. "O...m...g! No he didn't! I thought that you said I wasn't going to need my blade! Nobody disrespects my girl like that!" He said raising his voice causing a few people to turn around and look at them. "I will cut his balls off and stuff them in his no good mouth honey!"

"Calm down Xay." Kaliyah said in a hushed tone looking around. "He is a no body. I'll never see him again anyways it's just the nerve of him getting upset because I didn't want his broke ass! That's exactly why I prefer white men."

"Well...now I have to disagree with you there!" Xay interjected. "There ain't nothing better than a black man in the bed! I've had my fair share of black, white, Mexican, Puerto Rican, hell I've even had a Japanese before and I am telling you nothing compares to a brother! And on some real...thugs are the best! They puts it down!" He did a little booty popping move in his chair. "Honey, they will crack your back better than any chiropractor!"

Kaliyah erupted in laughter! "You are a hot mess Xay!" She replied still laughing and wiping tears from her eyes. Xay had made her laugh so hard that it'd brought tears to her eyes.

The server appeared at their table before Xay could respond. "Hello my name is Megan and I will be you all's server for today. Can I start you off with something to drink?"

"Yes, that would be great. I'll have a glass of Merryvale, Nappa 47." Kaliyah responded flipping her long wavy weave behind her shoulders and eyeballing the thin young waitress who looked to be in her early twenties. She eyed her from head to toe. *Never in a million years could I be caught dead in that getup serving motherfuckas.* She thought to herself, rolling her eyes as she continued to stare at the uniform that Megan was wearing and the shabby looking ponytail that she had her hair pulled back in. Her nails looked as if she'd bit them, they were all nibbled down to the tips of her fingers. Kaliyah cringed at the girl's appearance before glancing away in the other direction.

The server turned her attention on Xay. "I'll have the same."

"Very well, I'll be right back with your drinks." She told them before leaving.

Xay and Kaliyah continued to talk about Thrill while the server got their drinks. When she returned they both ordered the Moo Choo Chee, which was grilled pork tenderloin with light roasted red curry sauce, kaffir lime and green beans.

"So what did this guy look like? Was he yummy or fugly?" Xay inquired wanting to hear more about this guy that had Kaliyah's panties in such a bunch!

"Fugly?" Kaliyah repeated with wrinkles in her forehead, wondering what the hell Xay was talking about. He was always throwing around some new word that he'd made up.

Xay waved his hand. "Chile, I swear you are so slow! Fugly means fuckin' ugly! You are just adding the F from fuckin' and adding it to ugly!" He explained before taking a sip of his wine. "Now which one was he?"

Kaliyah shook her head waving her hand. "He was alright." She lied knowing that he was way more than alright.

"Hmph...I would probably have to see for myself. You know that your taste in men is horrible, most of the men that you go out with look like zoo animals."

"Whatever! I don't give a damn what you say. Their money looks damn good!" The two friends shared a laugh.

Xay gave Kaliyah a high-five. "And that's all that matters boo!"

Lunch was delicious but more importantly Kaliyah enjoyed talking to Xay. It took her mind off of the earlier incident that she'd had with Thrill. When she left the restaurant she went to the Marriot to meet Greg. She got the key from the desk and went upstairs to the room. When she got inside Greg was already naked and stretched out on top of the covers. He smiled when she came in, his hand stroking his little penis. Kaliyah smiled back as she sashayed towards the bed like she was walking down a runway. Inside she wasn't smiling at all. If it wasn't for the money she wouldn't dare put up with his little dick, no rhythm having, half-ass pussy eating, five minutes lasting ass! Fucking him was like watching paint dry...no watching paint dry was more exciting! She got no pleasure at all out of it. After the sex was when the real pleasure came. When he dug in his pockets and broke her off!

"Hey my chocolate kiss, Big Daddy has been waiting on you. He's been missing you." Big Daddy was the name that Greg had given his dick. She wanted to laugh so badly every time that he referred to his little nubby dick as Big Daddy! That was a big stretch of the imagination! There wasn't anything big about his dick except for it was a big disappointment!

"Hey, I've missed him too." She lied. She had a nice buzz from the three glasses of wine that she'd drink during lunch. She stood next to the bed and undressed slowly and seductively before crawling up on the bed with him. "Do you have condoms? If not I have some in my purse."

"I have some right here." He reached up under the pillow and produced three condoms, not that they would actually need three. He leaned over and kissed her nice and slow while fondling her breast and playing with her nipple. She moaned as if he was really turning her on.

"You like that don't you baby?"

"Mmmmm, yes you know I do daddy." The only thing that she liked was the fact that after she was done he would be making a nice deposit into her account.

"Lay back so that I can taste you. I've missed you so much these past two weeks."

She did as he had asked and lay back on the bed, spreading her thighs. "I've missed you too." Greg dove right in. She closed her eyes, hoping that he would be done soon. When she closed her eyes the weirdest thing happened. She saw an image of the guy from the gas station in her head and her pussy immediately became drenched. She opened her eyes back up really quickly!

What the fuck? She thought to herself. Why was she thinking about him and why was it turning her on. Greg was all over the place, he couldn't eat pussy worth shit! He found her clit and gave it a slight lick. She put her hand on his head. "Don't move, stay right there and keep licking that spot baby." She instructed. She closed her eyes again and again she saw Thrill. It was like something came over her body, her pussy started to throb and Greg's tongue actually started to feel good. "Oooh yes!" She screamed still holding onto his head. "Suck on my clit!" He did. She felt her climax starting to build, something that had never happened with Greg before. Actually in her mind it wasn't happening with him now because in her mind she saw Thrill's head between her legs as she gripped a hand full of his dreads. She locked her thighs on each side of Greg's head and came long and hard in his mouth. When she was done she released his head and laid there spent from one of the most powerful orgasms she'd ever had.

"You really did miss me." Greg said. She opened her eyes and saw him staring down at her with his face glistening from her juices.

She didn't even respond all that was going through her mind was what in the fuck had just happened. It had to have been the wine that had her thinking about Thrill.

Chapter Two

Thrill finished pumping his gas, then hopped in his car and drove off. He was still heated from the few words that he and Kaliyah had just exchanged. He drove to Wendy's and ordered him some food and then headed back to work. He owned his own customizing car shop, actually he owned three, one in Atlanta, GA, one in Albany, NY, and another one in Miami, FL. He was well paid but he'd never been the flashy type. He didn't try to keep up with what everyone else was doing, he just did him.

After he got back to work the rest of the day went by pretty fast. He got off around 7:30 and then went home. When he got there he took a nice hot shower, then got in bed and turned on the TV. It had been a very long day. All he wanted to do was kick back and watch Sports Center. He hadn't been watching TV but for ten minutes when his house phone rang.

He reached over on the nightstand and picked it up. "Hello."

"Hey, whatchu' doing?" It was Casey his ex-girlfriend. The two of them had broken-up over seven months ago but whenever she wanted to get her back blown out she always gave him a call. They'd broken up because she didn't have any drive or ambition. She was happy with her life just the way it was. She'd had the same part-time job at K-Mart for the past four years and she still lived at home with her parents at the age of 25. He'd asked many times if she would consider going back to school and getting some kind of degree, or find another job so that she could get a place of her own. Her reply was "You have money, why won't you get me an apartment with your stingy ass?" His reply was always. "I don't mind helping you or doing things for you but you have to be willing to help yourself." When he realized that she wasn't going to change he broke it off but being that he didn't like going around sleeping with a lot of different women and Casey's sex had always been the bomb he still hooked up with her from time to time.

"I ain't doing shit just laying here watching Sports Center. Why? What's up?" He asked already knowing what the purpose was for her call. He ran his hand down his flat washboard stomach.

"Stop playing boy you know what the deal is. I called for the one thing that I can get from your stingy ass!" She laughed. She was always making jokes about him being stingy but it never fazed him one bit.

"Boy?" He laughed. She knew that he was far from a boy. A boy could never do the shit to her body that he did. "Woman please you know that I am all man."

"I can't remember so can I come over and find out?" She asked hoping that his answer would be yes. She hadn't had any of his good sex in a while and her body was anticipating the pleasure that only he could give.

"Yeah you can come over." He replied laughing and shaking his head.

"What's funny?" Casey questioned.

"Nothing." Thrill lied. He was laughing at how thirsty she sounded.

"I'll be there in about 15 minutes, alright?"

"I'll be waiting." He hung up and turned his attention back to the television. Twenty minutes later he heard the doorbell. He got up from his bed and went to answer the door. He looked through the peephole and saw Casey standing there grinning like a Cheshire cat. She damn sure hadn't wasted any time getting there. He opened the door and stepped back to allow her to come in.

She came in wearing a tight short yellow and gold Coogie dress that hung off of one shoulder and barely covered her thick round ass cheeks. She was the color of milk chocolate with dark brown eyes, thin lips and slightly big nose. She was 5'9 and 160lbs. She was a really cute girl. Tonight she was wearing a long black wig with blonde tips. Thrill looked at her hair and shook his head before closing the door and locking it.

"What are you shaking your head for?" She asked defensively rolling her eyes as she turned and headed for his bedroom. She hated how he always seemed to be judging everything she did. That irked her nerves in the worst way!

"Nothing, I am just wondering what that is that you have on your head? You have beautiful hair so why do you cover it up with wigs that don't even look as good? I just don't understand." He admitted as he followed her.

"I just wear wigs for a different look." She huffed pulling her dress up over her head revealing that she wasn't wearing any panties or a bra. "Can we forget about my hair please?" She asked placing her hand on her hip. She'd come to get fucked not talk about her hair.

He didn't respond instead he picked her up and laid her back on the bed. He took off the pajama bottoms that he was wearing and climb on top of her in 69 position. She took the head of him in her mouth. He was so big in width and length that there was no way she could fit all of him inside of her mouth. Hell she had been fucking him for over two years and still couldn't take all of him in her pussy. She sucked and licked him until he was nice and hard. She could barely concentrate on the head that she was giving him because what he was doing between her legs with his tongue prevented her from doing so. He swirled his tongue around in her juice box before wrapping his lips around her clit and gently sucking on it. Her juices squirted out and she could feel them dripping down her ass. He licked and sucked her clit until he took her over the edge. Without missing a beat he got up and switched positions. He positioned himself between her legs and slowly worked the head of his massive penis inside of her tight opening. He fucked her with only the head for a few minutes trying to stretch her open some so that he could give her a few more inches. He only managed to get half of it in before she was begging him not to go any deeper. He fucked her nearly into a coma before pulling out and spilling his babies all over her stomach.

Covered in sweat, pussy throbbing from both pain and pleasure, Casey lay next Thrill trying to recuperate. Her legs were still trembling. He looked over at her and chuckled before reaching over on the nightstand and getting a cigarette from his pack. He stuck the fresh Newport between his lips and lit it. He took a long pull before inhaling the smoke and then releasing it through his nose and mouth. "Are you alright over there?" he teased.

"Fuck you!" Casey snapped. She knew he was being funny.

"You just did and couldn't handle it." He laughed. "It's a shame that after all this time you still can't take all this dick but you get an A for effort!" He rubbed her thigh.

"Whatever." She rolled over and began planting kisses down his chest and stomach. She continued her journey until she was face to face with his sleeping monster. First she teased it with her tongue, licking it, tasting her juices. Then she took him in her mouth and sucked him until she brought him back to life. Thrill finished his cigarette and then put it out in the ashtray. He reached down and pulled Casey up from where she was. She climbed on top of him and slid down as far as she could on his dick. "Oooooo...God...shhhh...iiiit!" She moaned.

He smacked her on the ass. "Take this dick girl!" He instructed a cocky grin covered his lips. He knew that he was blessed in the dick department and that his sex was off the chain. He'd never fucked a bitch that didn't come back for more...once she was able to walk again! He reached up and played with Casey's nipples and caressed her breasts as she rocked slowly back and forth. He placed both of his hands on her hips and pulled her down further on his dick and began grinding his hips in a circular motion.

"Oh shit!" Casey screamed as she felt him stretching her. It felt like he was ripping up her insides. "Thrill...Thrill...baby stop! I can't...this shit hurts!" She panted as she pushed against his chest. He ignored her and lifted his head taking one of her nipples in his mouth and gently biting it. He felt her juices squirt all over his dick. He continued getting his grind on nice and slow. "Mmmmm...Thrill...baby....mmmm...it still hurts." She moaned even though the pain had lessened some. He alternated between her nipples biting on them. Soon he felt her body tense up and then start to jerk violently. "Oh...shit...I'm cumming!" He was right behind her.

Thrill got up after the second round was over and went into the bathroom. He turned on the water in the shower while he took a piss. When he was done he hopped in the shower and washed up. He got out and dried off before wrapping the towel around his waist and going back to the bedroom. When he walked back into the room he saw Casey still balled up beneath the covers.

"Yo, what you doing?" He asked wondering why she was still in his bed instead of halfway home. "You need to get up."

Casey sat up propping herself up on her elbow. "What? Why you trippin'? It's late and I'm tired." She whined.

When she sat up he noticed that she'd even taken her wig off. His eyes landed on her hair lying on the nightstand. *Hell naw!* He opened up the top drawer of his dresser and took out a pair of boxers. He unwrapped the towel tossing it on the end of the bed. He put on his boxers and then slipped on his house slippers. "Look it's late and I have to get some sleep because I have to work in the morning. I'm not trying to be mean but you already know what it is. We fuck and you be on your way. You know we don't do the whole spending the night thing lil mama."

Even though that was how they got down his bluntness still hurt her feelings. "For real? So you really asking me to leave?"

"Come on man, don't do that." He replied becoming agitated. He couldn't understand why she was acting all shocked like this was something new to her.

"Whatever! It's all good. I'll leave!" She snapped flinging the covers back and hopping out of bed. Her pussy was super sore so she couldn't move as quickly as she normally would have. "I bet if I was Blake, I could spend the night!" She grumbled referring to the mother of his twelve year old son. She slipped on her dress.

Thrill didn't bother responding all he wanted was for her to hurry up and leave so that he could go to bed.

"See you don't have shit to say about that, do you?" She didn't give him time to reply. She answered her own question. "Nah because you know that I am right! You think that bitch is better than anybody else! That's why we didn't work because you were still hung up on her! Always comparing me to her and expecting me to be like her ass!" She went on and on until Thrill had heard enough!

"Will you please shut the fuck up?" He roared. "All I want is for you to take your ass home! You called me because you wanted to get fucked! I gave you what you wanted so what's the problem?"

"You's a rude ass mothafucka! That's the problem!" She stood with one hand on her hip and pointing at him with the other! "I don't appreciate you trying to play me like I am some random jumpoff!"

Thrill chuckled she could be so damn stupid at times! She never took the time to think before stupid shit poured from the hole in her face! "Oh I'm the one playing you like you are some random jumpoff but you called me to fuck?" He shook his head. "It's time for you to go. I really don't have time for this shit." He walked over and picked up her wig from the nightstand and handed it to her. "Here you go. Don't forget your pet." He chuckled.

She snatched the wig from his hands and rolled her eyes before turning and storming out of his bedroom and down the hallway. "Fuck you, Thrill! I mean that! I have no idea why I still fuck with your rude ass! You think that you are so much better than anybody else all because you have a lil money! Fuck you and your money!" She snatched open the door and stormed out not bothering to close the door behind her.

Thrill closed the front door and locked it. "Silly bitch and she wonders why I left her ass alone."

Chapter Three

Kaliyah took a sip from her wine glass. She was out with Paul tonight, one of her many sponsors. They were having dinner at Escorpion, a Mexican spot that she'd chosen. Tonight she was dressed in a black strapless Christian Dior dress that stopped mid-thigh. On her feet she had on a pair of silver Jimmy Choo sandals that tied up around the ankles. All of her jewelry was silver. She was wearing her jet black bob wig tonight. She knew that she was looking good because when she and Paul had come in several male heads turned even the ones that were with someone.

Paul sat across from her wearing a baby blue Calvin Klein button up and a tan pair of Calvin Klein khakis. On his feet he was wearing a pair of brown Calvin Klein loafers. He was a very attractive older gentleman. He had sandy blonde hair mixed with streaks of grey that hinted his age. He had hypnotizing emerald green eyes and a full beard and mustache, thin lips and a pointed nose. He was a little short for Kaliyah's taste, coming in at only 5'7 and about

197lbs. He had a great personality though and his sex was fairly good but most importantly his money was long just the way that she liked it.

They were eating their dinner and enjoying each other's conversation, when Kaliyah looked up and saw a familiar face being lead in their direction by the hostess. He was with an attractive young woman. She was tall and brown skinned and slim with small curves. She had thick jet black curly hair, rather big eyes, a small button nose and small lips. She was cute. She was dressed in what appeared to be a cheap white sundress and some white payless shoes. Kaliyah rolled her eyes at the woman's cheap taste in clothes. Where was her sense of style?

The hostess led Thrill and Monica to a table just across from where Kaliyah and Paul were seated. Kaliyah's eyes were glued to their every move. She nearly choked when she saw Thrill pull out the woman's chair for her. She was also surprised to see him dressed in a pair of dark blue Sean Jean slacks and a dark blue and white Sean Jean button up. She couldn't see his feet. His dreads were pulled back from his face tonight. She could see that he was very attractive but still not her type. He took his seat across from his date and the waitress came and took their drink orders. She had been so wrapped up in watching Thrill and his date that she hadn't heard Paul calling her name repeatedly.

"Kaliyah...Kaliyah...Kaliyah!" He called in an attempt to get her attention. He was starting to get a tad bit agitated by her rudeness. She seemed to be mesmerized by the couple that had just walked in.

Kaliyah tore her attention away from staring at Thrill and his date and redirected it on her date. "Yes Paul, I'm sorry. What were you saying?" She asked glancing over at the couple once again.

"Do you know those people?" Paul asked wanting to know what was so special about the couple across from them.

"No not exactly. I had a few words with that guy a couple of weeks ago."

"Oh well...do you want to leave?" Judging by the looks of Thrill, Paul didn't want any problems. He'd rather just leave.

"No, I'm fine." She replied picking at her food. So many things were running through her mind like, how was this thug able to afford a place like this? She wondered how much money did drug dealers rake in and how come he wasn't wearing any jewelry if he had money. Most drug dealers that she had seen that was getting big money owned lots of jewelry and tricked out cars. Granted he had been driving a nice car the day that she had seen him, it didn't scream big time hustler though. She'd pegged him for a small time nickel and dime hustler. Maybe she had been wrong about him after all. She glanced back over at the table where he was seated with his cheap date. This time he looked up and caught her looking at him. She quickly diverted her eyes and looked in the other direction.

It was too late though he had already seen her and he knew exactly who she was, the stuck up snobby bitch from the gas station! Her hair was different but he hadn't forgotten her face. She was breathtakingly beautiful. He'd never seen anyone who came close to looking as good as her and so it would've been impossible to forget her face along with her fucked up attitude. She needed to be brought back down to size and he was just the nigga to do it. He was confident about that.

He'd caught her staring in their direction a couple of times. Probably trying to figure out how he could afford an expensive place like the one they were at. Her dumbass should stop judging a book by its cover. He knew her type all too well. Her style screamed gold digger loud and clear. He knew that she would be all over him if she even thought that he had long paper. He laughed at his thoughts.

Monica looked over at Thrill skeptically wondering why he was laughing. "Are you okay?" She asked.

"Yeah lil mama, I'm good." He replied before taking a sip of his water.

Halfway through his meal Thrill looked up and caught Kaliyah looking in him and Monica's direction yet again. When she saw him look in her direction she rolled her eyes and turned her head. He leaned over and gave Monica a peck on the lips. "Will you excuse me for a second please? I'll be right back."

"Yeah sure." Monica replied thinking that he was probably going to the men's room.

Thrill got up and walked in the direction of Kaliyah and Paul's table. When Kaliyah saw him heading in their direction her heart rate picked up! *What in the hell was he coming over to their table for?*

When he reached their table, he looked at Paul and said. "What's up my man? I'm sorry to interrupt you all's dinner but your date keeps staring at me like she knows me or perhaps she wants to get to know me. I'm not sure which one it is but it's kind of rude!" He looked at Kaliyah. "I would think that she'd know that it is rude to stare. Ya know with her being so high class and all."

Kaliyah's mouth fell open. She couldn't believe that he'd had the audacity to come over to their table and say such bullshit. "Excuse you but who do you think you are coming over here to our table and interrupting our meal with this foolishness!" She was quite upset but she still managed to keep her voice down.

"It's not foolishness. Your damn eyes have been all over me since I walked in. Shit you were staring so hard that I could feel your eyes on me! Why don't you show this man some respect and keep your eyes on him and not me!"

Paul was at a loss for words. He'd felt some type of way by how Kaliyah had been staring at Thrill all night. He had even said something to her about it but she claimed that she was only looking because they'd had words before, which didn't make any sense. Him being the man that he was though, he felt that he needed to defend Kaliyah. He couldn't let this complete stranger just walk over and disrespect her even if she had been disrespectful the entire night.

"I'm sorry my good fella but maybe you should return to your table and leave me and my lady friend here alone before I have to call the manager and have you thrown out for bothering us. You see, the manager and I go way back and I'm sure that he would be very upset if he knew that you were over here bothering us. It is a free country so she can look anywhere she pleases." Paul leaned back in his seat feeling like he'd just done something big. He looked over at Kaliyah and winked.

Kaliyah looked at Thrill and smirked because she was sure that would shut his fuckin' mouth but oh was she wrong!

"Oh really? Well, let me just let you and your...ummm...lady friend is it?" He laughed. "Let me let the two of you in on a little secret. I go way back with Jose' also, probably further back than y'all as a matter of fact he is one of my regular customers so go ahead and call him out here. Or would you like for me to do it?"

Kaliyah looked from Thrill to Paul wearing a confused expression. Jose' didn't look like the type to do drugs but you never could really say who was doing what these days. Her mother had been on drugs for years and prostituting herself but the family swore they never had any indication that she'd been involved in anything like that because she hid it so well for years. She'd hid it until her drug habit had gotten so out of control that she didn't give a damn who knew what she was doing. She would've dropped to her knees and sucked a dick in front of the pastor if it meant getting what she needed to put in her arm or on in the end of her pipe!

Thrill reached in his pocket, Kaliyah and Paul both jumped. They both were afraid of what he might pulled out but to both of their surprise he pulled out a thick knot of money and peeled off three crisp one hundred dollar bills and threw them down in front of Paul. "Here you go my good fella." He said mockingly. "Go to Walmart and see if you can purchase yourself a set of balls because you obviously have none! Allowing this trick to sit here and disrespect you like it's nothing and then when I come over here and tell you to check her you gone fuckin' try and check me! Nigga you must be smokin'!" He shook his head and then looked at Kaliyah. "Yeah it's good that you is stuck up and wouldn't give me any play because if you tried some shit like that with me! I would leave your triflin' ass right here and hell no, I wouldn't pay for shit that your ass ate! I would tell you to pay for it or let the nigga that you been staring at all night pay for it. You'd better stick with these square ass niggas that you fuck with because a real nigga would break your ass down!" He looked at Paul one last time and laughed before walking off.

Kaliyah was so embarrassed that she wanted to disappear! She'd never had anyone talk to her that way or put her in her place like Thrill just had. She was speechless for the first time in her life she didn't even have a slick comeback! Even if she would've had one she would've been too afraid to voice it! She grabbed her clutch off the side of the table. "Are you ready to go?" She asked Paul.

He looked puzzled. To be honest he was ready to leave but when he'd asked her before if she was ready to leave she'd said no. Now she was ready to leave. Not only that but the Kaliyah that he'd known for the past five months didn't back down from anyone. That was what had attracted him to her in the first place, her sassy attitude and the way she seem to run things. His wife had always been a push over and it was a turn off. So when he'd met Kaliyah she had reignited that fire inside of him. Her take charge attitude always took him over the top in the bedroom. He loved the way she dominated him and told him exactly what she wanted and demanded that he give it to her! The Kaliyah sitting in front of him was not the one that he was used to. This stranger had her visibly shaken and if he wasn't mistaken a little turned on. He had seen that lustful look in her eyes enough times to know it when he saw it. She could say what she wanted but there was more to her and this guy than she was letting on.

"You're ready to leave because he came over here?" He couldn't hide his annoyance. "I thought that you weren't going to allow him to chase you out of one of your favorite restaurants."

"I am not allowing anyone to chase me anywhere!" Kaliyah snapped rolling her eyes and wondering why he was asking her questions instead of calling over their waitress and getting the check so they could leave! "I am leaving because I want to! Now will you please pay for the check and take me home!" She sucked her teeth and shot a nasty look over in Thrill's direction. He didn't even notice because he was too wrapped up in the conversation that he and Monica were engaged in.

"Oh so now you want to go all sista-girl on me but when that thug came over here the cat had your tongue! And what do you mean take you home? We have some unfinished business to attend to." He reminded her.

He must've bumped his head! Kaliyah thought to herself. After the way Thrill had just humiliated her, sex was the last thing on her mind! "I don't feel up for it tonight, maybe some other time. Now, I am going to ask you again, will you please pay for the check and then take me home!" She looked at him and waited for him to answer.

By now Paul was fuming. He waved the waiter over.

"Yes sir what can I do for you?" The waiter asked when he arrived at their table. He looked over at Kaliyah and gave her a polite smile, thinking to himself that she was a very lovely lady and wishing that he could afford to entertain someone as lovely as her. She looked at him and rolled her eyes. The smile he was wearing quickly faded.

"Can you bring us the check please? And if you don't mind could you split it. I'm only paying for my meal and she will be paying for her own." Paul said looking at Kaliyah. His entire face had turned a bright shade of red. If he wasn't getting any pussy she wasn't getting a free meal and she damn sure wasn't getting in his car! She could hitchhike back across town for all he cared!

Kaliyah's mouth fell open when she heard what Paul said to the waiter. She couldn't believe it! She wanted to breakdown and cry so badly but she knew that she couldn't. She'd already suffered enough embarrassment in one night to last her a life time! "Are you serious?"

"Yes...dead serious." He turned his attention back to the waiter. "That will be all thank you."

The waiter disappeared to go and do as Paul had asked. As soon as he was out of hearing range Kaliyah asked Paul. "What is your problem? I know that you don't expect for me to pay for my own meal! Don't tell me that you are taking the advice of some drug dealer!" She raised her voice.

"Maybe I am. Maybe I'm not. Who's to say? But the one thing that I will tell you is that you had better find yourself a ride home since you are so upset over that *drug dealer* that you can't have sex tonight!"

The waiter returned with two separate checks. Kaliyah opened her purse and whipped out her credit card and handed it to the waiter. Paul did the same. The waiter disappeared again and a few minutes later he returned with the receipts for them to sign. They signed and then they both got up and walked out. The waiter looked at the table and couldn't believe his luck when he saw the three crisp one hundred dollar bills. He hurriedly scooped them up off the table and stuffed them in his apron.

Outside Paul gave the valet his ticket so that he could go and retrieve his car. Kaliyah took out her cell and called a cab. They told her that it would be a fifteen minute wait. When the valet returned with Paul's car he hopped in and pulled off screeching tires.

As Kaliyah stood there waiting for her cab she felt so stupid. She had never been so humiliated in her entire life but she promised herself that it would be the last! She thought about calling up Xay and asking him to come pick her up but she knew that he would ask a million and one questions. She really didn't feel like dealing with that and she also didn't want him to know how she had been humiliated, not once but twice in one night. She looked behind her and through the glass window she could see a clear view of Thrill and his date. They were laughing and enjoying their dessert. He was even feeding the clearance rack shopping bitch! She could feel anger and jealousy both boiling over inside of her!

As much as she wanted to deny it something about this thugged out stranger turned her on in the worst way. Ever since the first time that she had ran into him at the gas station she couldn't get him out of her head. Damn he had even started to invade her dreams. Whenever she was having sex with one of her sponsors their faces would become his and her hormones would kick into overdrive and she would experience orgasms more powerful than she'd ever experienced before. Tonight when he had stepped into the restaurant walking like he owned the motherfucka she had been so turned on that she had to keep crossing her legs underneath the table and squeezing them together to try and calm her kitty kat down. There was no denying the fact that she wanted this man to dick her down in the worst way! But first things were first there was no way that she was going to allow him to sit up in there with that off brand chic and eat dessert after he had ruined her date and caused her to have to pay for her own meal and call a cab for a ride home! Oh hell no not Kaliyah! She turned and walked back into the restaurant. The hostess greeted her as she came back through the door.

Chapter Four

"You're back again I see. Did you forget something?" The middle aged Caucasian man dressed in black slacks, a white dress shirt, burgundy vest, black bowtie and black shiny dress shoes asked her. He prayed that she wasn't returning for the three hundred dollars that'd been left on the table.

"As a matter of fact I did. I will only be a minute!" With that she stormed past him, her Jimmy Choo sandals making a loud clicking noise with every step that she took in Thrill's direction!

Thrill spotted Kaliyah just before she made it to his table. He smirked because he knew that she was on her way over to make an even bigger ass out of herself than she already had. He knew that she was upset because he had peeped the exchange of words between her and ol' boy when he left their table earlier. He could tell by the expression on both of their faces that they hadn't been words of endearment. He had really been shocked when he'd looked out the window and seen her still standing there and her date was nowhere in sight. Ol' boy must've had bigger balls than he'd thought.

When Kaliyah reached the table where Thrill and Monica were sitting she put her hands on her hips. "I guess you feel like you did something big by coming over and ruining my evening! I don't know who in the fuck…"

Thrill held up his hand to cut her off. "First of all, I don't know who in the fuck told you that it was cool for you to walk over here and start screaming at me like you pushed me out of your fuckin' womb or some shit shawty but if you know what's good for you you'll pipe the fuck down." He said never raising his voice because he felt no need to but even as calm as he was speaking his words held enough venom that she got the point. "Second of all, I didn't ruin shit. You need to get some respect about yourself and learn that if you are with one nigga eating off of his dime then you shouldn't be choosing the next nigga wit your damn eyes. That man did right by leaving your ass here. Don't no man want a bitch who don't have no respect about herself. Now if you don't mind will you please get the hell on about your business so that I can finish eating my food? I mean damn, just a few weeks ago your stuck up ass didn't have any words for a *thug* like me. You said that you only talk to *real men.* So go and find yourself a *real man* and stop bothering me and mines." He looked across the table at Monica who was wearing a proud smirk on her face like he had just preached the gospel.

Kaliyah was speechless but she pulled it together quickly. "Go fuck yourself!"

She turned to walk away but Thrill stopped her. "Yo shawty just for the record, as far as your little comment about only talking to real men. Baby girl, I am the realest nigga you will ever meet!"

"Just for the record...again go fuck yourself!" She replied and then stormed back out of the restaurant and just in time too because her cab had just arrived. She hopped in the backseat and told the driver her address.

During the drive to her house she laid her head on the back of the seat and exhaled. She was so upset with Thrill that she wanted to cry but she had refused to let him see her do so. Now in in the back of the cab and away from the restaurant she finally let her tears flow freely. Why did it seem like he was out to take her down and why was she allowing him to affect her this way? For goodness sakes she didn't even know him! She swiped at the tears that were rolling down her face. She was fuming! She wasn't as mad with Thrill as she was with her own self. How could she be attracted to someone who was so cocky, disrespectful, and sold drugs for a living? What the hell was happening to her? She had never even been interested in someone like him so why now? Regardless of the sexual attraction that had her craving for a taste of his thug passion she promised herself that she would do everything to push Thrill out of her mind.

As soon as she made it through the door of her apartment she kicked off her sandals and flicked on the lights. She dropped her keys on the coffee table and then went upstairs to her bedroom where she stripped out of her dress and laid it across the chaise at the end of her bed. Her body was demanding a nice long hot soak in the tub. She walked into the bathroom wearing nothing but her black laced bra and panty set from Victoria Secret and put the stopper in the tub. Then she turned on the hot water and mixed in a little bit of cold and then she poured in some of her vanilla scented bubble bath. She left out of the bathroom while the tub filled with water and went back downstairs into the dining room where she had a mini bar. She got herself a glass and fixed herself a double shot of Ciroc and tossed it back. After the night that she'd just had she needed that and then some. She poured herself another shot to take upstairs with her. When she got upstairs she sat her drink on her dresser and took off the bobbed wig that she'd been wearing. She placed it on the mannequin head that was sitting beside the mirror. She took off the wig cap and placed that on the dresser. She ran her hands over her head full of tight reddish-brown close cut natural curls. She was dropped dead gorgeous and looked even more beautiful with her natural hair than she did with all of the different wigs that she wore. She unclasped her bra and pulled off her panties, leaving them in a pile on the floor. She picked up her drink and walked back into the bathroom and turned off the water. Stepping into the tub, she sat down and laid back relaxing her head back on her bath pillow. The hot water felt like heaven to her body.

****

Meanwhile, Thrill and Monica were just making it back to her place. He'd known her for a little over seven months and they'd gone out on a few dates but they'd never slept together. It had crossed both their minds quite a few times but they'd both remained patient because neither of them were sure of what direction this thing between them was headed. So far they'd been going with the flow but he knew that it was going down tonight by the way that she'd been extra flirty throughout the evening, touching him every chance that she got. When he'd walked her to the door she had insisted that he come in, so he did.

He was seated on the sofa waiting on Monica. She'd told him that she was going upstairs to change into something a little more comfortable. He really didn't see the point in her changing clothes when he was going to take them right back off of her anyway. Monica was a little on the slim side she wasn't thick like he preferred his women but she was really cute and had a nice little body. His thoughts were interrupted when she walked back into the living room. She was wearing a red sheer cami with red sheer panties to match and a pair of clear stilettos like strippers be wearing. She was looking really sexy and without any clothes on her ass looked a little bit bigger. His dick immediately swelled in his pants.

"Damn girl you looking good enough to eat." He complimented her as she made her way over to the sofa where he was sitting and straddled him. When she sat down on his lap a very unpleasant smell invaded his nostrils. It was so foul that it literally made him gag.

"Are you okay?" Monica asked with a concerned look on her face as she locked her arms around his neck. Thrill stood up with her still on his lap, nearly dropping her. She caught herself and stood to her feet. "What is it?"

"Is that you smelling like that?" He hadn't meant for it to come out in such a harsh tone but how else was there to say it?

Monica looked insulted and embarrassed. She placed her hand on her small hip and stepped back looking him up and down. "What the fuck do you mean is that me smelling like that?" She snapped.

"I'm not trying to be rude but I didn't smell it until you sat on my lap. Didn't you smell it?" He asked knowing damn well she had to smell the odor that was coming from between her legs if he did.

"No! I don't smell shit!" She lied quickly. This wasn't the first time that a man had told her that her pussy smelled foul but she really liked Thrill and hearing this come from him really cut her deep. She didn't understand why she had such a strong odor emitting from her pussy. She bathed every day and wore clean underwear. She didn't sleep around and she douched regularly. So what was the problem?

"You're right you didn't smell shit because shit smells better! Baby girl you need to go get a pap smear or something because something ain't right with your shit! I ain't trying to make you feel bad or anything like that but there ain't no way that you and I can do anything with you smelling like that and that's real talk." He started to walk towards the door.

"Oh so, you are just going to walk out on me just like that? The smell ain't even all that damn bad!" She really didn't want him to go. She'd heard several rumors about what he was packing and she wanted some of it bad! Most dudes still hit it even after knowing that she smelled so why was he trippin'.

Thrill looked at Monica in disbelief. He couldn't believe the words that she'd just allowed to slip from her lips. "Maybe it ain't that bad for some niggas but it is for me. I don't just put my tongue or my dick up in anything."

She reached out and touched his chest and he stepped back. "Thrill, don't do this. I really like you a lot..."

"Monica, this ain't about how much you like me or how much I like you. This is about your personal hygiene. I apologize if I hurt your feelings but I'm not the type of nigga who bites my tongue. Shawty, you need to see a doctor or something...real talk."

"All women have a little bit of an odor, it's natural."

"What?" He asked hoping that she didn't seriously believe the bullshit that had just come out of her mouth. There was nothing natural about what he'd just smelled. "Monica, you are a nice woman and I really like you a lot but until you handle whatever it is that you have going on down there..." He pointed down towards her crotch. "We can't do anything."

Tears filled her eyes. Her feelings were crushed. "So does this mean that you don't want to see me anymore?" She dreaded the answer that she knew was coming.

"I don't know...maybe we can still chill. Holla at me sometimes." He replied turning and heading towards the door.

In a last attempt to keep him from leaving she blurted. "What if I just give you some head?"

Without even stopping or turning around, he answered. "Nah lil mama, I'm good." With that he was out.

Monica flopped down on the sofa sobbing loudly. She knew that it was over between her and Thrill. How could she have allowed him to slip right through her fingers like that! *Fuck!* She cursed herself.

Chapter Five

Kaliyah stepped out of the tub and dried off. While she was in the tub she'd gotten a craving for some Krispy Kreme donuts and since there was a Krispy Kreme's right up the street from her she decided that she'd run back out and get her a box of hot donuts. There wasn't nothing like some fresh hot donuts to make a chic feel better when a nigga had plucked her nerves...well at least not for her. Krispy Kreme donuts were her guilty pleasure. She slipped on a short pair of shorts and a cami, not bothering to put on any underwear. She put on some deodorant and some vanilla scented body spray and grabbed her wallet and her keys and left. When she got to the Krispy Kreme there was a nice line but she wanted her donuts and so she took her spot in line behind a gentleman.

She heard him mumble. "Damn this line is long as hell."

"Hmmm tell me about it." She replied. The gentleman standing in front of her turned around and it was none other than the asshole that had ruined her night! She hadn't even paid any attention to what he had on or that he had dreads. "Oh my goodness! Are you serious? Damn, I can't get away from you for shit!"

He had to look at her for a second before he realized who she was because her hair was different. "Damn shawty you look different without your hair on!"

Kaliyah looked confused for a second before she caught on to what he was saying. "Whatever." She started to walk off.

"What are you leaving for? I ain't gonna bother you!" He promised while admiring the way that her ass jiggled in those little shorts that she was wearing.

She didn't respond she just kept on walking. She didn't even want to be in the same space with him, not after the way that he had embarrassed her earlier. She couldn't take any more of his rudeness tonight!

He followed her outside. "Wait up a second. Damn you running like I am the big bad wolf or something!" He laughed.

Kaliyah stopped and turned around. "Why do you want me to wait so that you can embarrass me again or make me look like an ass in front of all of these people here too?" She said waving her arms as she spoke.

"Nah it ain't even like that." He admitted. Truth was he thought that she was mad pretty but she just had a fucked up attitude. He had only treated her the way he did earlier because of the way that she had come off on him the first time that they'd met. He felt like now she may have learned her lesson and decided to try and bury the hatchet. Plus he wanted some of what she was switching in those little Juicy shorts bad! He'd been physically attracted to her since the first time that he'd laid eyes on her at the gas station. Even though she tried to act like she wasn't feeling him, her eyes were telling a totally different story. She wanted him just as bad as he wanted her. "I'm sorry for the way that I treated you earlier but to be honest you deserved it."

"What? Are you serious?"

"Yes, I'm serious." He replied mockingly. "That day at the gas station you looked at me and talked to me like I was beneath you but tonight when I walked into Escorpion. You couldn't keep your eyes off of me, like I was a different nigga other than the same one who had tried to introduce myself to you at the gas station. You were so into me and what I was doing that you couldn't even pay attention to the man that you were with when all you had to do is stop being stuck up for two seconds and tell me your name the day that I had first asked you and you wouldn't have been sitting there with his lame ass staring across the room at me. Instead you would've been with me." He spoke confidently and that turned her on. She liked his boss-like attitude. She'd never had a man or anyone for that matter speak to her that way. Most men groveled at her feet and jumped through hoops in hopes of getting next to her. Hell, there had even been a few women who'd done the same and if their money was right she'd served them just as quick as the men.

"How do you figure that I wanted to be with you?" Kaliyah questioned smacking her lips and still trying to fake like she wasn't feeling him.

"Woman do you ever stop playing games? I ain't no little ass boy and I have been around long enough to be able to tell when a woman is feeling me. Besides the eyes never lie and your pretty grey ones are telling on you big time." She rolled her eyes. "Tell you what…let me pay for whatever you are getting to make up for messing up your date."

Kaliyah pretended to think about it and then replied. "Okay that is the least you can do for being such a pain in my ass."

"You ain't seen nothing yet." He responded suggestively while licking his lips. He let her walk ahead of him as they reentered Krispy Kreme. *Damn she phat as hell! I am going to enjoy that!* He thought to himself.

"Stop looking at my ass." Kaliyah said over her shoulder.

"Stop switching it so hard or better yet you shouldn't have worn those little ass shorts. You want somebody to look at your ass." He told her matter-of-factly.

She didn't bother responding to his last comment. *Lord what are you doing even socializing with the dude, Kaliyah? After all of the humiliation he put you through earlier? What is wrong with you?* She chastised herself. She had no idea why she was feeling this dude. He was so not her type but the way that he carried himself was slowly but surely winning her over.

"By the way my name is Thrill." He introduced himself from behind her in line. "I told you before but you at the gas station that day but I'm not sure if you remembered. Are you finally going to tell me yours or is it still not interested?"

Kaliyah looked back at him and then turned back around. "Yep."

Thrill laughed. "It should be 'liar' because you're definitely interested but I see you like to play games. I guess because you are so used to having niggas chase you. Don't get me wrong, you're fine as hell but not fine enough for me to be acting all thirsty behind your ass. That ain't what I do." He reached in his pocket and pulled out two crisp twenty dollar bills. "Here you go." He handed them to Kaliyah. "Enjoy your donuts."

Kaliyah took the money from his hand and he turned and headed for the door. "Where are you going?" She asked confused because she'd thought that he was going to order something as well.

Thrill stopped walking and turned around. "I don't have time to play games, gorgeous and I see that's what you are about. I thought maybe you'd learned that from our last two encounters but obviously not. You need to stick to fuckin' with lames because you couldn't handle a real nigga like me anyways." He turned and pushed the door open and walked out.

By the time he reached his car Kaliyah was right on his heels. "You know what I am so sick of you!" She screamed! "Why do you have to be such an asshole? I see that you're the type who gets mad when things don't go your way. So just because I didn't tell you my name, you gone get mad and leave? You really need to grow up!"

Thrill opened his car door to get in. "I ain't mad shawty. You're the one out here screaming and shit, causing a scene." Kaliyah looked back and noticed a small group of females staring in their direction pointing and laughing. "I'm simply going on about my business. I tried to be nice to you but you still want to act all stuck up and shit. That's what's up. I just don't have time for it. Now enjoy your donuts and the rest of your evening." He got in his car and left, leaving Kaliyah standing in the parking lot fuming.

Chapter Six

Kaliyah sat outside next to the pool in her backyard with her cell pressed against her ear. She was engaged in a heated discussion with Greg about the same thing that they'd been going back and forth over for the past three months.

"Kaliyah, she's my wife! Can't you understand that? She's sick and she needs me to do all that I can for her. Wouldn't you want the same thing if it were you?" He pleaded.

Kaliyah rolled her eyes and smacked her lips. She honestly didn't give a damn about his wife or her illness! All she wanted was for him to stop spending all of his money on medical bills and expensive treatments trying to cure her cancer! He'd told her when they met that his wife had stage five brain cancer and the doctors had told him that she didn't have long. To her it made more sense to save his money and just let the bitch die! The doctors had done all that they could do for her, so why keep spending unnecessary money when it was already a known fact that she was going to die anyways?

"Honestly, no I wouldn't want you to keep spending money on all of those different doctors and expensive medicine when I already know the outcome. Every doctor has told you the same thing! To me what you are doing is pointless!" She didn't care if her words came out harsh or cold! She was upset because he'd promised her a trip to Cancun and had yet to make good on that promise! Every time that she brought it up his excuse was he couldn't afford it at the moment because of his wife's medical expenses. That was exactly the reason she felt he should let her die and collect the insurance money! That way she could go on her vacation and he wouldn't have that burden anymore! To her they both could benefit from it!

Greg sat at his desk unable to believe that someone could be so heartless and also unable to believe that he'd fallen for someone like her. When he'd first started messing around with Kaliyah it was all about the sex. He'd needed something to take his mind off of his wife's illness but as time went on she'd become something more to him. He enjoyed being with her. She made him feel alive, more alive than his wife of seventeen years ever had. He loved his wife, Madeline, but if it wasn't for her illness he would've been left her for Kaliyah! His plan was to stay by her side and do whatever he could for her until she passed. That way he would feel less guilty about his affair with Kaliyah. He'd also planned to ask Kaliyah to marry him once Madeline passed but now he was questioning whether or not that would be a good idea. He'd experienced her bad attitude and foul mouth on numerous occasions but never like today. All of the mean and venomous things that she'd said during their conversation he knew he wouldn't ever be able to forget.

"Kaliyah, it isn't pointless. I am trying to give her as much time as money can buy. We have children! Even though they are grown it doesn't make it any easier on them losing their mother. It seems to me that you would be able to understand that. What if it were your mother?"

Kaliyah let out a chuckle. "Hmph, my mother has been dead to me for a very long time so if it were my mother I wouldn't give a damn." She answered truthfully as she thought about how Nettie had abandoned her years ago for the streets. She'd never even known her father because Nettie had slept with so many different men to support her habit that she had no idea who impregnated her. She knew that she wasn't all black but she wasn't exactly sure what other race she was mixed with. That was about all she knew of her father is that he wasn't a black man. "Listen Greg, obviously you have a lot going on. So you go ahead and deal with your wife and her health issues. I hope everything turns out well but I don't have time to hang around while you place me and my needs on the back burner for her."

"What? Are you breaking things off between us?" He asked his voice cracking. He really didn't want to lose her. "Kaliyah please don't do this? Not right now. I need you..."

"Good bye, Greg." She cut him off and then disconnected the call turning off her phone because she knew that he would only try to call her back, begging and pleading.

"You are one cold bitch!" Xay giggled as he took a sip of his sangria. He was stretched out on the pool chair in the pool, a pair of Dolce and Gabbana shades covered his blue eyes. "Honey, you are worse than the devil himself!"

Kaliyah slipped her shades back on and lay back in her seat. "Call me whatever you want! I don't have time to waste! My time is money and if he can't afford it then it's on to the next! I didn't get all of this..." She waved her arms around referring to her home. "...by feeling sorry for men and sticking by them through their trials and tribulations! Screw that!"

Xay laughed at his best friend, she was truly an evil bitch but he admired how she kept it one hundred regardless of how anyone felt about her. "I hear you girl. So how are things with you and Kent? Do you still have his pathetic ass thinking that he is the only one?"

"Yep. He just bought me this $6,000 ankle bracelet." She stuck out her ankle so that Xay could get a good look. He sat up and removed his shades so that he could inspect the piece of jewelry around her ankle. "I'd say that things are pretty good."

"Get it diva! And Paul...what's been going on with him?"

"Paul has been out of town for the past few weeks on business." She lied. The truth was that he hadn't called her since the night that he'd left her at Escorpion's. "We've talked on the phone and of course he's been keeping my bank account fat but we haven't seen each other."

"Well that's good. Your pussy needs a break because I swear that thing has more miles on it than American Airlines!" Xay teased.

"Hmmm maybe so but as long as I get paid I am going to continue to sling this nookie!"

"I know that's right!" He laughed. "Chile, I forgot to tell you. I was with Cohen the other day. He'd asked me to take him to pick up his Mustang because he just had some work done to it. He had it repainted and got the interior redone. Anyways we went over to a customizing shop over of 117th Street. Honey, I thought that I'd died and gone to chocolate heaven! I know that you say you say you prefer white men but diva if you ever step foot in that place you will definitely change your mind! I have never seen so many fine brothers in my life. I was damn near drooling at the mouth. Cohen had the nerve to get an attitude saying that I was disrespecting him by looking at other men right in front of him." He took off his shades and sat up on the pool chair. "I didn't pay him any attention. I enjoyed the view the entire time that we were there! The finest one of them all though was the owner! Chile, I've fantasized about his sexy ass since I saw him. The entire time that he was talking to Cohen about his car, I was wondering what his dick would taste like in my mouth!"

Kaliyah nearly choked on her drink! "Ewwww Xay!"

"Bitch please! As much dick as you suck! What the hell you ewwwing about?" He checked her real quick before continuing his story. "He was downright yummy! Skin the color of dark chocolate with these sexy full kissable lips and a banging ass body! His voice was fucking hypnotizing! He could talk to me all night honey!"

Kaliyah shook her head at Xay. He was always going crazy over some guy! Every week he'd seen the finest man in the world. "Well did you go back and get his number?"

"Nah, he's straight."

"How do you know? He could be a DL brother."

"Nah, I could tell. Trust me, I can tell when a man has some suga in his tank and Mr. Thrill didn't. He likes fish! His eyes were glued to some heffa's ass that had come in after me and Cohen. She was switching around in some lil coochie-cutters. He could barely finish going over all of the things that he'd done to Cohen's car for looking at her. She wasn't even all of that!"

Thrill, owner of a customizing shop! No, it couldn't be the same Thrill but the description is definitely accurate and there couldn't possibly be two men named Thrill in Atlanta! Kaliyah thought to herself. She needed to know more. "Are you sure his name was Thrill?"

"Yeah...that's what was stitched on his shirt."

"Did he have dreads?"

"Yes honey!" His eyes rolled up in his head as he recalled in his head how sexy Thrill had looked with his dreads hanging lose the day that he'd seen him. "Hold up...how did you know that?"

Kaliyah ignored his question and asked another of her own. "And you said that he was the owner?"

"Yep that's exactly what I said." He responded still wanting to know where all of these questions were coming from and how she knew Thrill. "What's up with the interrogation?"

"Nothing." Kaliyah replied her wheels were now spinning. *The owner of a customizing company...that's how he could afford Escorpion's but that still didn't mean his money was long. There was only one way to find out!*

"You said the shop was on 117th St.?"

"Look heffa stop asking me questions unless you plan on answering mines!" Xay snapped. "How do you know Thrill?"

"He's the asshole I told you about that I had words with at the gas station about a month ago. I don't know him but we've bumped into each other a couple of times since then." She informed him an evil grin on her lips as she thought about the information that Xay had just divulged to her. "I had no idea that he owned his own business though. He has a fucked up attitude but I might be able to work around that depending on the size of his bank account."

Xay shook his head. "You don't even like black men. Chile, you'd better slow your role before your thirsty ass ends up in a morgue!"

"Well if I do I'll be the flyest bitch there!" Kaliyah laughed and so did Xay but he'd been serious about what he said even though she'd taken it as a joke. He'd been thinking for a while that she needed to slow her role some before she ran across the wrong man but he knew that she was going to do whatever she wanted regardless of what he or anyone else said. "Anyways, you are talking about me. You'd better stop gawking at every man you see before Chen goes upside your head or worse, downgrade your ass back to that studio apartment that you were living in before he put you in that nice ass condo that you are staying in now."

"I'm not worried about Cohen downgrading any damn thing! Besides, who says that Cohen was the one who put me in that condo?" He asked, lips pursed.

Kaliyah took off her shades and sat up eyeing her friend. "Uh-uhh, I know that you haven't been holding out on me? Is there someone that you haven't told me about?"

"A girl isn't supposed to tell all of her secrets." He giggled taking a sip of his drink and winking at her before slipping his shades back over his eyes.

Chapter Seven

Kaliyah gave herself one last glance over before grabbing her keys and heading for the door. She was looking and feeling like a million bucks as she hummed Sponsor on her way to the car. She had a breakfast date with Kent this morning and then she was off to the car shop over on 117th St. to see how much it would cost to have her car painted. She giggled as she thought back to how she'd used her key to put several long nasty scratches down the entire passenger side of her car. She'd needed an excuse to show up at Thrill's shop. She opened her car door and tossed in her Marc Jacobs bag before sliding into the driver's seat of her pink 2012 Chevy Malibu.

When Kaliyah arrived at Ria's Bluebird, Kent was already seated at a table near the window. As the hostess led her over to him she noticed that he was on the phone. Once she had reached the table she gave him a light peck on the cheek and then took her seat across from him. From the sound of things he was on a business call. She picked up the menu and began browsing over it. After another few minutes of giving instructions to whoever was on the other end of the phone Kent hung up.

"I apologize, sweetheart for being so rude." He told her as he leaned over and pecked her on the lips. "You are looking lovely as usual."

"Thank you." She blushed.

The waitress came over. "Good morning. Are you two ready to order." They both ordered banana pancakes and fresh fruit. The waitress left to go put in their orders. While they waited for their food they engaged in small talk.

"So how has your week been?" Kent asked Kaliyah as he ran his fingertips up and down her arm. He absolutely adored her. It was about more than the sex for him. He found her to be one of the most beautiful creatures that he'd ever laid eyes on. She had her flaws but he had his fair share as well. The fact that she accepted him for him was what made him so crazy about her. She never judged him. He sat there looking at her thinking to himself that one day he was going to make her his. He'd thought about it countless times before but now in this moment staring at her he knew that one day he definitely wanted to settle down with her and only her. Right now he wasn't ready but when he was he planned to file for a divorce from his wife and marry Kaliyah. She didn't make him feel like Kaliyah did. He was no longer in love with her and he hadn't been for a while. To be perfectly honest the two of them were no more than roommates. He did his thing and he was more than sure that she did hers, which he didn't mind as long as she did it in the streets and not in their home. They had two teenage sons together and he wanted to wait until they were both grown and out of the house before he left. That wouldn't be much longer because their youngest was sixteen.

"It's been alright. I can't complain." Kaliyah answered as she took a sip of her water. "I haven't been doing much just hanging around the house."

"Really? That doesn't sound like you. Something must be wrong. Talk to me, what's going on? Maybe I can help." He offered still rubbing her arm.

Kaliyah went into actress mode, tears filled her eyes as she looked up at him. She knew how much he hated to see her cry. "I've been doing a lot of thinking lately. Mostly about my mother and I think that it's starting to take a toll on me." She swiped at the fake tears that fell from her eyes. "I know that it probably shouldn't matter to me anymore that she isn't in my life being that she hasn't ever really been involved in my life but for some reason it does. I just want her to get clean and try to work towards establishing some type of relationship with me. Does that sound crazy?"

He reached up and wiped her tears with the back of his hand. "No beautiful, that doesn't sound crazy at all. Every child wants their parents to be involved in their lives. No matter how old you get you're always going to want the love and support of your parents. Nothing can take the place of that love. I totally understand." His heart went out to her. He'd never seen this side of her before. Normally she was all hardcore but right now she was fragile and vulnerable.

The waitress returned placing their food in front of them. "Is there anything else that I can get for you?" She asked trying not to stare at Kaliyah but wondering if everything was alright.

"No thank you." Kent told her. "We're fine, thank you."

Still feeling a little uneasy by seeing Kaliyah crying, she asked. "Are you sure?" Her eyes were on Kaliyah.

"Yes, we're sure." Kaliyah assured her as she dried her eyes. The waitress gave her a sympathetic smile and then left the two of them to enjoy their meal.

"So is there anything I can do to make you feel better, beautiful?" Kent asked shoveling a forkful of banana pancakes into his mouth. "You know, I love seeing a smile on that beautiful face of yours. I've never seen you like this before and I don't like seeing you like this."

Kaliyah continued to pick at her food like she'd been doing for the past five minutes. She stared at her pancakes like they were venomous. She let out an exaggerated sigh. "I don't know. I think that I need to get away for a few days to kind of take my mind off of things and clear my head."

Kent sat his fork down. "Where?"

Kaliyah looked at him pretending to be confused. "Where what?"

"Where would you like to go?" He asked. "Name a place."

That's what the fuck I'm talking about! She smiled on the inside proud of how easily she'd been able to fool him. She knew how he felt about her and so she used that to her advantage. "Anywhere?"

"Yes, anywhere. Name a place." He repeated.

She pretended to think about it, and then she replied. "Cancun, I've never been there before and from the pictures that I've seen it's absolutely breathtaking."

He reached in his pocket, took out his wallet and handed her his American Express card. "Here you go. Enjoy yourself and do whatever it takes to put a smile on that beautiful face of yours."

She wanted to burst out laughing in his face but decided to stay in character. "Are you sure?" She hesitated like she didn't want to take the card from his hand.

"Yes, I'm sure." He smiled placing the card in her hand. "I will do anything to make you smile woman. You know that I am absolutely crazy about you." He told her meaning every word of it. Something about her was downright addictive, which was why he couldn't imagine not having her in his life.

"Thanks, I really need this." She took the card and put it away in her pocketbook before standing, leaning across the table and planting a wet kiss on his lips. "I really appreciate this." She kissed him again and then sat back down.

"No problem. I've never seen you so upset before and I don't like it at all. You go down to Cancun and enjoy yourself, try to forget all of your worries at least for the time that you are there. I wish that I could come with you so that we could make love in the sand while listening to the waves crashing against the shore." He smiled and took a look at his watch. "I have a couple of hours before I have to go into the office. What do you say we get out of here and go somewhere where you can do a few things that will put a smile on my face?"

He smiled at her suggestively.

Damn it! I should've known that he would want some pussy! Oh well for what he is spending on this trip and the shopping spree that Xay and I are going to go on, he deserves it. Kaliyah thought to herself as she looked across the table at the sucker who'd just fell for her bullshit sob story and handed over his credit card. What men would do for a beautiful face and a shot of pussy was just downright pathetic!

Forty-five minutes later, Kent was on all four in the middle of a king-sized bed at the Ellis hotel with his face buried in one of the fluffy pillows on the bed. He was biting on his bottom lip with his eyes squeezed shut as he enjoyed the feel of Kaliyah's wet tongue on his asshole. The pleasure that she was giving him should've been illegal. That was another reason why he couldn't leave her alone and he gave her whatever she wanted. She did any and everything that he wanted. Nothing was ever too overboard.

"Mmmm...yeah...mmmm...that feels so fucking good!" He moaned as one of his hands worked feverishly stroking his stiff organ. "Put the plug in and then bring your pretty little ass here so that I can fuck the shit out of you!" Kaliyah did as she was told and inserted his anal plug. Then she crawled on the bed. "Lay on your back. I want you looking up at me with those pretty eyes while I'm inside of you." She did. He lifted her legs placing them over his shoulders before entering her to the hilt. Between the plug in his ass and the tightness of Kaliyah's warm wet pussy, he was in sheer heaven. He pumped in and out of her all the while staring deep into her eyes. It didn't take long for him to reach his climax. He rolled off of her and lay on his back staring up at the ceiling.

Kaliyah got up, went into the bathroom and took a quick shower. She got dressed and then used one of the toothbrushes and toothpaste provided by the hotel to brush her teeth. When she was done she went back out into the room to find Kent still in bed but on the phone. He was engrossed in a heated conversation. From what she could hear he'd promised someone that he'd be somewhere and they were upset at the fact that he hadn't arrived.

"I told you, I'll be there and I will! Don't call my phone again with this nonsense! Know your position!" He barked into the phone.

She picked up her pocketbook and keys before walking over and giving him a peck on the cheek. "I have to run." She whispered. "I'll call you later."

He nodded his head to acknowledge that he'd heard what she'd said. She exited the room feeling like she'd accomplished a lot in the past few hours but there was still important business to be handled and it had to be done before she left for Cancun. She got in her car and headed in the direction of 117th St.

Kaliyah walked into Black Custom's, her heels clicking with each step she took. She was a woman on a mission. She walked up to the service desk and was greeted by a short brown skinned brother rockin' a short fro.

"Hey pretty lady." He smiled looking her up and down taking in her flawless beauty. He'd never seen anything like her in person, maybe on TV or in a magazine but never up close and personal. "What can I do for you? Your wish is my command." He licked his lips suggestively still eyeing her.

I hope he don't think he's impressing me with that bullshit! She rolled her eyes behind her shades before removing them. She looked around and then back at him. "I am looking to have my car painted. Somehow, I ended up with several long scratches down the passenger side of it."

"When were you trying to have it done?" Jamal asked brainstorming a way to get her attention in his head. He could clearly see that she wasn't interested but he desperately wanted to change that before she walked out of the shop.

"As soon as possible..." She let out an exaggerated sigh. "Ugggh, I can't bear to drive around in it any longer with those awful scratches along the side of it."

Jamal leaned over the counter, trying to make eye contact with Kaliyah. "Don't stress yourself beautiful. I could get on that first thing in the morning for you. I had a few other customers ahead of you but I can see that you really want your car taken care of so for you I can move a few things around and slide you right in." He licked his lips again smiling at her. "How's that?"

"That sounds good but are you sure your boss doesn't mind?" Instead of allowing him to answer, she asked. "As a matter of fact, may I speak to whoever is in charge here? I'm not trying to be rude or anything but I am about to go out of town in a few days and I would really like for my car to be painted by then. I can't afford to take your word that you can move people around and paint my car and it hasn't even been cleared by your boss." She looked at him giving him a serious look to let him know that she wasn't there to flirt. She was about her business all other bullshit could wait!

Jamal straightened up feeling slightly offended by how she'd dismissed everything he'd said. He cleared his throat. "I'll get him for you."

"Thank you." She reached in her purse and took out her compact mirror glancing at her make-up and hair to make sure that everything was intact. If the owner really was Thrill she wanted to be looking her best. A few of the other guys that worked there were checking her out on the low. She acted as if she didn't notice. *Yeah, I know I'm a bad bitch but y'all can't afford this. All you can do is window shop.* She thought as a few of the guys waved in her direction, some winked, and some even mouthed the words 'call me'.

Jamal walked to the back and knocked on Thrill's office door.

"Come in." He heard him call from the other side of the door.

He turned the knob and pushed the door opened. Thrill was sitting at his desk going over some paperwork. "Hey there's a chic out here asking to speak with the boss." He informed Thrill.

Thrill looked up from what he was doing, wrinkling his brow and raising one eyebrow. "Why, what's wrong?"

"She wants us to paint her car because it has some scratches or something along the passenger side. She says that she needs it done ASAP and I told her that I could get on it tomorrow morning for her but I would have to move some people around…"

"Move some people around?" Thrill was confused as to why Jamal was telling some chic that he would take her in front of other customers that he'd already made commitments to. The more that he thought about it, he knew why...Jamal would do anything for a bitch! He was one of those niggas with no game at all so he'd promise a bitch the moon if he had to just to get her number! "Nah man, tell her if something becomes available you will give her a call but you can't just go putting her in front of other people."

"I feel you but man if you saw this chic...Thrill, you would move a few motherfuckas out the way for her ass too! She's bad. I'm talkin' Janet Jackson, Halle Berry bad!" He thought about how sexy Kaliyah was looking in the pink strapless dress that she was wearing and the way that it was hugging her every curve. He really wanted to go back out and promise Kaliyah that he'd paint her car. He'd never pulled anything that looked like her and even though she was acting all stuck up, he felt like he still needed to give it his best shot!

Thrill shook his head. "Man, you will walk barefoot across hot coals just to get a chick's attention! Let me share something with you, sometimes less is more. Meaning that sometimes you need to relax and stop acting like you've never seen a woman before. When they see you doing all that extra shit it's a turn off for most women."

Jamal really wasn't trying to hear the shit that Thrill was spitting. He felt like it was easy for Thrill to sit back and talk that shit because he had money and women seem to fall at his feet! "I hear you but..."

Thrill got up from his desk. "Don't worry about it! I'll tell her myself!" He walked past Jamal and out of the office. As he approached the front desk he noticed that there was something familiar about the woman waiting. He chuckled to himself as he got closer and noticed that it was none other than Ms. Fucked Up Attitude!

Just as Thrill approached the desk, with Jamal tagging along behind him, Kaliyah looked up. *It is him!* She tried to pretend like she was shocked and at the same time annoyed to see Thrill. "Oh my goodness, somebody please tell me that this is some kind of a joke!" She rolled her eyes and looked around pretending to be looking for the owner. "I don't have time for games. Where is the owner?" She shifted her weight for one foot to the other and placed her hand on her hip.

"You're looking at him." Thrill replied in a no nonsense tone. Though he was kind of glad to see her, he made it a point not to let it show. She'd proven that he couldn't be nice to her. "How can I help you?"

"Are you serious?" She continued to play like she didn't believe that he was the owner.

"If there is one thing that you should have learned from the past few times that we've bumped into each other, it's that I don't play games. I apologize if you are disappointed to find out that I don't sell drugs. You should learn to stop judging a book by its cover." He told her. "Now again, how can I help you?"

Jamal stood next to Thrill listening to the exchange of words between the two. He was curious to find out how they knew each other. *Ain't this bout a bitch! Besides money, what does this motherfucka have that I don't?* He questioned in his head. The common disease known as jealousy that he suffered from flare up.

Jamal thought of himself as a decent looking cat. He didn't think he was ugly by far and to be honest he wasn't. His cinnamon brown complexion and light brown eyes were very attractive. He wasn't very tall, standing only 5'5 inches and he could've stood to work out a little to tighten up the beer gut that he'd developed but he was still far from ugly. He dressed nice and kept his fro and facial hair trimmed real nice. He wasn't lazy, kept a job and would do anything to make his woman happy…when he had one. So he couldn't understand why the women that he went after wouldn't give him any play.

"I'm trying to get my car painted because it has some really ugly scratches along the passenger side, which I am sure he already told you." She pointed in Jamal's direction all the while never taking her eyes off of Thrill.

Her grey eyes trying to read his expression, she was trying to figure his mood. She didn't want to say the wrong thing and set him off. The plan was to come here and hopefully change his opinion of her so that she could get to know him a little bit better and learn his financial status. "The thing is, I am planning to go out of town the beginning of next week which is only four days away and I would like to have it done before I leave."

Thrill logged onto the computer behind the desk and looked over the schedule to see if there was any way that he could fit her in before then but they were all booked up. That wasn't a surprise because they always stayed busy. He was the man to see in Atlanta when you wanted anything done to your ride. "Nah...shawty, I'm sorry but we are all booked up for the next two weeks." He said still looking at the schedule and shaking his head. He finally lifted his eyes from the computer screen and looked up at Kaliyah. "If you leave your name and number someone could give you a call if something becomes available though. That's the best that I can do."

She smirked. "My name and number, huh?"

"Yeah, how else am I going to let you know if something becomes available?" He looked at her like she was stupid.

She started to laugh. "I'll tell you, you don't give up easily do you?"

A confused expression covered Thrill's face. "What are you talking about?"

"You know exactly what I am talking about." She wasn't laughing but still smiling. "You've asked me my name twice and I said no both times so I guess you figure that I have to give it to you now."

Thrill turned and started to walk off. He didn't have time for her dizzy ass. He could tell that niggas like Jamal had really fucked her head up!

"Where are you going?" Kaliyah called after him confused.

He stopped walking and turned to face her. He took a few steps back in her direction so that he wouldn't have to speak loudly. "I'm going back to my office. I don't have time for high school bullshit! You came here to have your car painted and I don't mind doing that for you. As a matter of fact, I was trying to figure out a way to make it happen but you are so full of yourself that you think I am trying to game you out of your number. You are a beautiful woman but your attitude really takes away from your beauty. You have to be one of the most ignorant people I have ever met." He turned to walk off but she stopped him.

Even though she was slightly embarrassed and offended by his words she didn't let it show. "Damn, calm down I was only joking with you. Don't you have a sense of humor?" He didn't bother to respond he just stood there silent, waiting for her to say what was on her mind. Seeing that he wasn't going to reply, she continued. "Listen, I really want my car painted and I would really appreciate it if you could do it for me. Hopefully within the next few days, I know that you said that you were booked for the next two weeks but everywhere else that I've been to have a longer waiting period than that." She lied, taking a small notepad from her pocketbook and a pen she scribbled her name and number on it. She tore the piece of paper off and handed it to Thrill.

He took the piece of paper, looking at the name and number scribbled on it. "I'll give you a call if something becomes available."

"Thank you." She gave him a warm smile.

"No problem." Kaliyah turned and sashayed out of the shop. He stood and watched her admiring her beautiful body until she was out of sight.

Long after Kaliyah had left the shop, Jamal couldn't stop thinking about her. He couldn't stop picturing those alluring grey eyes in his head or her gorgeous smile. He stood behind the desk fantasizing about what it would be like to have someone like her on his arm to show off to all of his boys. He could just imagine the jealous stares that he'd get. A smile formed on his lips.

"Jamal...Jamal!" Scooter, one of the other guys that worked at Black Customs, called. "Man, wake yo ass up!"

Hearing Scooter's voice ripped him away from his thoughts, Jamal looked up. "I wasn't sleep, I was thinking about something. What's up?"

"Nothing, I came to ask you if you'd already taken your lunch break." Scooter replied playing with the loose change in his pocket.

"Nah, I haven't." Jamal answered. "You about to go out now?"

Scooter laughed at the dumbass question that he'd just asked. Why else did he think he was asking him if he'd taken his lunch break? "Yeah, I'm going to run down to KFC. You want to ride with me?"

"Yeah, hold on. I'm going to ask David if he can cover the front for me until I get back."

"I'll be in the car."

On the way to KFC, Jamal talked about Kaliyah nonstop. He told Scooter how beautiful she was and how he'd give anything to be with a woman like her.

Scooter shook his head. "You don't even know that hoe! What you mean you would give anything to be with a woman like her?"

Jamal looked over at Scooter and then back out the window. "You know what I mean. I mean, a woman as beautiful as her. She looks like a damn angel. I swear that woman's beauty if fuckin' hypnotizing."

Scooter turned up the radio in an attempt to drown out Jamal. He was sick of hearing about Kaliyah. He didn't care if Jamal didn't like it! If he said something about it his ass would be walking back to work. He was acting worse than a teenage girl with her first crush!

Chapter Eight

After leaving Black Customs, Kaliyah stopped at the Shell station up the street from the shop to get something to drink. She parked and got out to go inside. Just as she was about to go inside she heard someone call her name.

"Kaliyah, what are you doing over on this side of town?"

She didn't have to turn around to know who it was. She closed her eyes cursing under her breath. "Shit! I have the worst fucking luck in the world." Opening her eyes she turned around slowly. Standing there on the end of the sidewalk in a pair of cut of jean shorts, an old faded yellow t-shirt, a pair of old dirty sneakers and a scarf half tied around her nappy hair, was Nettie. She was now walking in her direction.

"What are you doing over here?" She repeated. She looked as if she hadn't slept in a few days and Kaliyah noticed that she was missing her two bottom front teeth.

"I came over here to try and get my car painted at the shop down the street." Kaliyah told her trying to ignore the awful smell emitting from her mouth. Her breath was sickening.

"Oh, you talkin' bout the one that them black boys own?"

"Yes…" Kaliyah rolled her eyes. She had no tolerance at all for Nettie. She tried her best to avoid her at all cost. In her heart, she didn't have a mother. Her mother had died years ago. She looked at the dried up figure in front of her and felt ashamed. How could she be related to someone like this?

"Them some fine mens up in there child! I sho' wouldn't mind getting a lil piece of one of them!" Nettie laughed and tried to touch Kaliyah on her arm but Kaliyah snatched away looking at her like she was contagious.

"Look, I have to go." Kaliyah opened the door to the store to go in.

"Okay…do you have twenty dollars so that I can get me something to eat?" Nettie asked eying her daughter, she knew that Kaliyah didn't want to give it to her but she didn't care what she wanted. All she cared about was her handing over the money so that she could go find Chief and get her a hit. She also knew that Kaliyah didn't care for her at all and it hurt but not enough for her to kiss her ass to try and have a relationship with her. She'd tried on several occasions to try and establish some type of relationship with her but each time Kaliyah pushed her away. Treating her like she was beneath her. She realized that she'd made a lot of mistakes as a mother but it wasn't because she didn't love her daughter. It was because the call of the streets and drugs had been too strong for her to ignore. She'd tried hard, even gone days and sometimes even weeks without doing any drugs but each time the cravings for the poison would win. She was sick. She had an addiction. An addiction that she'd had for years. It wasn't something that she could just kick. What she truly needed was a support system. Someone there to help her, encourage her and not give up on her but who? Everyone in her family had turned their backs on her years ago, washed their hands and given up, including her daughter. The streets and the drugs were truly all that she had left. No one knew the loneliness, guilt, and depression that she suffered when she was sober. Only she knew her pain. In this moment now standing face to face with her daughter no one could possibly understand how it felt to have her own child look at her with her nose turned up. It was hurtful.

"Nettie, I am not giving you any money! You know better than that!" Kaliyah was annoyed at the fact that every time Nettie saw her she asked for money. She wasn't surprised because she'd known that the question was coming. Why couldn't she ever see her and not ask for anything but just be happy to see her? "Look they have hotdogs and microwavable sandwiches in the store that you can eat. I will buy you something to eat and pay for it myself but I am not going…"

"I don't need you to pay for shit like I'm a fuckin' child!" Nettie all but shouted, her little neck swiveling side to side! "I can pay for it my damn self all I need for you to do is give me the money!"

Kaliyah looked around embarrassed by the scene that Nettie was causing. "Will you please keep your voice down?" She snapped in a hushed tone. "I am not going to give you any money! You and I both know that you aren't going to buy any food with it."

Nettie snatched the Marc Jacobs bag that dangled from Kaliyah's shoulder! "I don't need you to give me shit!" She ripped the bag open and flipped it upside down pouring all of its contents onto the ground!

The cashier at the counter had seen everything that had just transpired between the two and rushed to the door. "Do you want me to call the police?" She called to Kaliyah.

"No ma'am, she's m-m-my…no don't call the police." Kaliyah replied too embarrassed to say that the crackhead who'd just snatched her pocketbook was her own mother. Kaliyah looked at Nettie who was now bent over reaching for her wallet. She didn't bother trying to stop her because she knew that was a fight that she couldn't win. She figured she'd just let her have the hundred and twenty some dollars that was inside. Maybe she'd smoke enough crack to OD and die!

Nettie picked up the pink wallet that was lying on the ground in the pile of things that she'd dumped from Kaliyah's purse. She opened it up and took all of the money that was inside and then tossed it back on the ground. She stood up stuffing the money in the front pocket of her dirty shorts. "You can call whoever you want to call bitch!" She yelled to the young cashier who was still standing in the doorway watching. The young blonde haired girl turned and went back inside assuming that she may be safer inside. Nettie turned her attention back to Kaliyah, she'd kneeled down and was picking her things up putting them back in her bag. "You should've just given me what the fuck I asked you for in the first gotdamn place." She purposely kicked the rest of the items that were still on the ground and sent them scattering across the pavement. She waltz off across the parking lot and across the street still talking shit. "Ol stuck up ass! Done forgot where you came from! Trying to act like you are all of that! Got the nerve to try and look down on me like you are better than me! Bitch, I know all about you. You ain't nothing but a prostitute. Selling yo' pussy to them rich white mens and suckin' their little dicks!"

Kaliyah kept her head down and continued to pick up her things. She ignored her mother's harsh words and warm tears streamed down her cheeks. *And people wonder why I am such a bitch.* She thought to herself. She finished picking up her things and then left. She didn't even bothering going inside the store. She was too embarrassed after having everyone witness the altercation between her and Nettie. She drove out of the parking lot wiping tears from her eyes. She hated Nettie with everything in her. She'd never been a mother to her. She'd abandoned her years ago giving her away to her aunt and uncle. They'd raised her until she was fifteen, which was when she'd packed a few clothes in a bag and left. After years of having her aunt's husband molest her, she finally couldn't take it anymore. She'd moved in with her boyfriend, who was seven years older. He'd taken care of her and provided for her until she was able to provide for herself.

She continued swiped at the tears that were rolling down her cheeks. She was so upset that she could barely concentrate on the road. When she finally made it home, she tossed her bag and keys on the sofa and headed straight for the minibar in the dining room. She didn't bother to get a glass. She just screwed the top off the bottle of Patron and took it to the head. She took it with her into the living room and flopped down in front of her computer. She went online to purchase the tickets for her trip to Cancun. She decided to call and check with Xay to make sure that he would be free to go before purchasing the tickets.

She picked up the cordless phone and dialed his number. He picked up on the third ring. "Hey diva!" He answered.

"Hey, I was calling to see if you wanted to go with me to Cancun?"

"Ummm...hell yeah! Bitch, what kind of question is that? Who wouldn't want to go?" Xay screamed his perky high-pitched voice hurting her ears. "When do we leave? I need to go shopping! I am going to have to hit up Cohen's ass for some dough! I have to be fly strutting my fine ass up and down Cancun!"

"Don't worry about shopping we can go tomorrow. Everything's on me." She let him know.

"Awwww...shucks now! I can't do nothing with you bitch!" Xay was screaming into the phone! "I want to be just like you when I grow up!"

She forced a laugh. "I hear you. Look, I am about to purchase these tickets and then take my ass to bed. I am tipsy and have a slight headache. I've had a long day."

He could hear in her voice that she wasn't in the best mood. "Alright diva, give me a call tomorrow then."

"Okay, I will." She hung up and then purchased their tickets. When she was done she took a shower and went to bed.

Chapter Nine

Thrill pulled up to Blake's house just as the sun was starting to go down. He peeped the new black Mercedes Benz parked in her driveway and shook his head because he already knew that she'd wasted more money on a new car. Blake had a thing for cars. She'd get a new car every few months if he didn't say anything. Majority of the time he didn't say anything because he felt that after all of the shit he'd put her through in the past she deserved any and everything that money could buy.

He stood on the step and rang the bell. He could hear her heels clicking against the hardwood floor in the hallway as she made her way to the door. That was another thing, she loved heels. He couldn't remember a time when she wasn't in them.

Blake looked through the peephole and saw Thrill. She unlocked the door and swung it open. "Before you say anything, I only got it because the truck burns too much gas." She lied knowing that he was about to get on her about buying another car. He'd just bought her a Cadillac truck for her birthday three months ago. She tucked her long blonde hair behind her ear and chewed her bottom lip nervously as she waited for him to start his sermon about her wasting too much money on cars.

Thrill walked in past her without saying a word because he knew that she was lying. He also knew that in a few more months something else would be parked outside so there was no use in going back and forth with her about it. He walked down the hallway to the kitchen and opened the refrigerator and took out a beer. He twisted the cap off and tossed it into the trashcan before taking a seat at the island. The smell of food invaded his nostrils. "What are you cooking?" He asked.

"Lasagna, toss salad, cheesy garlic bread and I have a cheesecake in the refrigerator." She answered before putting on an oven mitten and opening the oven to check her lasagna. Thrill sat watching her and admiring the woman that she'd become. She'd become so domestic, cooking, cleaning, baking and she was very involved at Tyreke's school. She was definitely the one that got away. If he could turn back the hands of time and undo all of the shit that he'd put her through in the past he would. Back when they were together he'd chosen to run the streets and sleep with nasty bitches over being a family man. His run in the streets ended when he got caught along with two other guys robbing a gun shop. Though he was only the driver of the car the judge still didn't hesitate to slap him with five years. During those five years, he had a lot of time to think about all of the things that he'd put Blake through and the fact that he was missing out on the first years of his son's life. Tyreke had been only six months when he'd gotten locked up. Blake was loyal the entire time and remained faithful. She was right there every weekend, her and Tyreke, for five whole years. He promised her that when he got home he would do right by her and get a real job. He promised her that he was done with the streets and he'd made good on that promise. When he came home he got a loan from his cousin Taz and opened up Black Customs. As the business grew in Atlanta, he decided to open the shop in Albany and then the one in Miami. His brother Jay ran the shop in Albany and his cousin Eric ran the one Miami. They were all doing really well. He'd even opened up a strip club in Atlanta, which Blake ran for him. Everything that he owned her name was also on it. In his eyes she deserved half of everything because she'd stuck by his black ass when no one else had and because she was the mother of his one and only child. If he could, he'd give her the world without any hesitation. He cursed himself every time that he saw her and realized how stupid he'd been to come home from prison and cheat on her after she'd stuck by him through a five year bid. To make matters worse the bitch that he'd cheated on her with ended up giving him chlamydia and he'd given it to Blake which was how she'd found out about his unfaithfulness. He really felt like a dumbass for allowing such a good woman to get away chasing behind something that hadn't been worth his time. He let out a sigh and shook his head as he admired his beautiful babymama.

Blake was Caucasian with long blonde hair that hung midway of her back. She had ocean blue eyes and a smile that could light up a room. The thing that Thrill had fallen in love with when he first laid eyes on her was her dimples. She had the most adorable deep dimples that he'd ever seen. She was petite with an athletic frame. She worked out faithfully to keep her body in top shape and it showed. Carrying Tyreke had thickened her up in the hips and thighs and it looked good on her.

"So why are you in here cooking all of this food?" Thrill asked taking a swig of his beer. His eyes roamed over her body as he waited for an answer.

Blake closed the oven door and took off the oven mitten and tossing it on the counter. She turned to face him. "Our son does have to eat, doesn't he?" She asked her glossy pink lips forming a smile as she eyed Thrill. She knew that he still had it so bad for her and it was kind of cute but she knew that no matter what she could never go back there. He'd caused her entirely too much pain. She'd moved on and found someone who truly did love her and showed it by being faithful and putting her first. Though Thrill couldn't stand her being with someone else he was always respectful towards her fiancé Cameron and she appreciated that because she knew that it was hard for him having to see her with someone else even though it was his fault that they were no longer together. She was proud of the man that Thrill had grown into but it had come too late. He had to lose her before he'd chosen to grow up and realize what was most important.

Thrill nodded his head. "Yeah, I guess. Where is he anyways?"

"Upstairs in his room. He was playing the game. I'm not sure what he's doing now." She watched as Thrill rose from his seat and turned the beer that he'd been drinking up to his lips. He drank the remainder of what was left in the bottle before tossing it into the trash.

"I'm going to go up and kick it with him for a while."

"Okay."

"By the way, I like the new whip."

"Thank you." She smiled.

He left her in the kitchen and went upstairs. When he got up there he knocked on Tyreke's door and waited for a response.

"Yes...who is it?" Tyreke called from the other side of the door.

"It's your pops."

"Come in."

Thrill pushed the door and went inside. Tyreke was seated on the floor next to the bed with a game controller in his hand, eyes glued to the TV screen. "Hey pops." He spoke without taking his eyes off of the TV.

Thrill took a seat on the bed. "Start a new game so that I can whoop your butt in a game real quick."

For the first time since Thrill had entered the room, Tyreke took his eyes off of the TV. Thrill was speaking his language. "Pops come on now, you and I both know that ain't about to happen." He stood and restarted the game and then tossed Thrill the other controller. He took his seat back on the floor where he'd been sitting before. "I hope that you took your heart medicine because the whoopin' that I am about to put on you might cause you to have a heart attack at your age." He clowned his dad. The two of them had a really close relationship and Tyreke enjoyed every moment that they spent together. He often wished that his mom and dad could get past whatever issues it was that they had and get back together. Cameron was okay but he preferred his mom and dad together.

"Boy, you talk a lot of smack. You must get that trash talking from your mama." Thrill teased back as he reached over and ruffled his hair. Tyreke had a big curly afro that he normally kept in braids. Today it was loose. "Let's see if you can back all of that trash talking up. Better yet, put your money where your mouth is." Thrill reached in his pocket and took out two hundred dollars and laid it on the bed. "What's up?"

Tyreke stood up and coolly strolled over to his dresser. He reached inside of his top drawer and pulled out two crisp one hundred dollar bills. He closed his drawer and walked back over to the bed placing his money on top of Thrill's. "Let's do this."

Thrill couldn't do anything but laugh and Tyreke joined in. That was definitely his boy. "Boy, you are something else." The two of them began playing the game.

Downstairs, Blake sat at the island watching the 51inch Plasma TV that was mounted up on the wall. She heard Tyreke and Thrill yelling, she smiled shook her head. She knew that they were playing the game. She was used to this. She raised her cup to take a sip of her iced tea and the doorbell rang. She already knew who it was. She got up and went to the door and peeped through the peephole. Cameron was standing there on the other side of the door looking like he'd just stepped off the pages of GQ. She unlocked the door and opened it.

"Hey sexy." He smiled taking off his shades so that he could get a better look at his beautiful woman. "Damn, you look sexier and sexier every time that I see you."

"Don't I though?" Blake blushed doing a slow little spin so that he could get a really good look at her in the pair of blue jean shorts and backless top that she was wearing.

"Come here woman." He grabbed her and pulled her into his arms. He leaned down and kissed her soft lips. At first it was just a simple kiss but the longer they kissed the more passionate and intense it became.

"Mmmm..." Blake moaned coming up for air. "Now that's how a man is supposed to greet his woman."

"Well, there are a few other ways that I'd like to greet you." His hands moved down the lower part of her back and then slipped down to her round backside. He palmed both of her cheeks giving them both a gentle squeeze.

"Let's go upstairs."

"We can't...Tyreke is awake and Thrill is up there with him. Their playing the game." She noticed the unpleasant expression that covered his face when she mentioned Thrill. She knew that he didn't care much for Thrill but she'd let him know from day one that was her son's father and he could either deal with him being in the picture or keep it moving. She couldn't for the life of her understand why Cameron acted so insecure whenever Thrill was around. She'd never given him any indication that there was still something between the two of them because there wasn't and Thrill was always respectful towards him whenever the three of them were in the same space. Maybe it was just the fact that they were exes and he felt uncomfortable knowing that the two of them had once been in a relationship. Whatever the reason she didn't feel it was necessary because he had a past as well and she didn't feel threatened by any of his exes. "Come on." She unwrapped his arms from around her waist and took him by the hand pulling him into the house.

"How long has he been here?" Cameron asked. His entire demeanor had changed. The smile that he'd been wearing when she'd first answered the door was now gone and she could hear the agitation in his voice.

She let go of his hand and pushed the door closed, rolling her eyes up in her head. She let out a frustrated breath. "Why?" She asked turning to face him. She didn't feel like being interrogated about Thrill. This was the only complaint that she had when it came to their relationship. "Why does it matter how long he's been here?"

"Because I want to know? Is there a problem with me knowing?" He asked staring at her. He knew that Thrill still had it bad for Blake and even though she'd told him several times that there was nothing between the two of them and that she was happy with him. He still wasn't one hundred percent sure that she was completely over Thrill. The two of them were a bit too close for comfort. He loved Blake and could truly see himself with her for the rest of his life but he wasn't so sure if he could deal with the close relationship that she and Thrill had. He didn't understand why Thrill couldn't just come by, get Tyreke and be out. Instead he would come by and chill for hours. Sometimes he felt like an outsider as he sat back and watched Thrill, Blake and Tyreke. They were like one big happy family and he was...just there.

Blake shook her head, her long hair swaying from side to side. "Cameron, we are not going to do this every time that Thrill comes around." She told him. "He came here to see his son, which he has every right to do."

"Whoa, hold up." He held up his hand to stop her. "I never said that he didn't have a right to come and see his son. I just asked how long has he been here and the next thing I know you are getting all upset and defensive. Is there a reason why you are so defensive?"

"Yep, there sure is. I'm getting defensive because yet again you're acting all insecure because Thrill is here. You act like you don't trust me and I don't like that shit at all. I haven't given you any reason to treat me that way and I don't appreciate it. I don't question you about Rasheeda or Jamie."

"There is no reason for you to question me about them. They don't hang around my crib like he does yours. They come over and drop the kids off or pick them up and be on their way. There's a big difference in my relationships with them and yours with him." He explained. He could tell by the expression on her face that he'd pissed her off and that she wasn't trying to hear shit that he had to say. He hadn't meant to start an argument or make her feel like he was accusing her of anything. He just wanted her to try and see things from his point of view. Thrill was always around and he wasn't feeling it. He let out a sigh. "Just forget that I said anything."

"Yeah...let's do that." Blake snapped and brushed past him heading back into the kitchen. Instead of following her, Cameron went upstairs to the bedroom and lay across the bed.

Chapter Ten

Xay and Kaliyah strolled through the mall sipping on raspberry lemonade and talking. They'd met up so that they could buy a few things for their trip which was only three days away.

"Girl, I am about to cut up in Cancun!" Xay squealed, he was super hyped about their trip. "Honey, I am going to be laid up with a different man every night! I think it might be a good idea for us to get separate rooms!"

Kaliyah shook her head and ran her freshly manicured fingers over her head of curls. Today she was sporting her natural hair. "Lord have mercy, you are about to get out there and act like a straight up whore!"

Xay stopped in his tracks and removed his shades from his eyes. "Heffa please don't sit up here and try to front like you are going to be in Cancun acting like a nun. Shit, you can't even keep your knees together here. Imagine how you are going to act once you get out there. I bet it ain't nothing but a bunch of old wealthy freaks out there just waiting to spend a couple stacks for some fresh young tender booty!"

Just as Kaliyah was about to respond her phone rang. She took it out of her bag and looked at the screen. A number that she didn't recognize was flashing on the screen. She pressed send and answered. "Hello."

"Yeah, is this Kaliyah?" His smooth baritone voice poured through the receiver.

"Yes, this is she." She responded a smile playing on the sides of her lips. Xay watched intensely as his friend's entire demeanor changed after answering the phone. Kaliyah immediately recognized Thrill's voice and she also knew the reason for his call.

"I was calling to let you know that we can paint your car for you. A customer didn't show this morning so that freed up a spot." He explained. "Do you think that you can bring it by 1:00?"

"Yeah sure." She nodded her head as if he could see her through the phone. She'd already turned and started towards the exit. Xay was on her heels wondering where in the hell she was going. They'd only bought a few pairs of shades and some sandals. "Thank you so much. I can't began to tell you how much I appreciate this."

"You don't have to thank me Shawty. I'll see you when you get here." Thrill told her.

"Okay." Kaliyah took the phone from her ear and ended the call. She put her phone back inside her bag and began fishing around inside for her keys.

"Where in the hell are you going? Why are we leaving?" Xay questioned as he followed behind her trying to keep up. All of a sudden she was speed walking. The sandals that he wore made it difficult for him to walk fast because of the slippery bottoms.

"I have to go home and get the Malibu so that I can take it to the shop." Kaliyah said over her shoulder. She found her keys just as they reached her car and pressed the remote on the keychain to unlock the doors. She popped the trunk and tossed in her bags.

Xay tossed in his bags as well and then got in the car. Once they were both inside, he took off his shades and turned in his seat so that he was facing Kaliyah. "Bitch, spill it!" He knew her like the back of his hand and he could tell that her scheming ass was up to something.

Kaliyah drove out of the mall parking lot and into traffic. "What are you talking about Xay?" She tried to play dumb like she had no idea what he was talking about.

"Why does the Malibu need to go to the shop? And why are you so damn excited about getting it there? And what shop are we talking about?" He eyed her suspiciously as he interrogated her.

They came to a stoplight and Kaliyah glanced over at Xay who was still turned in his seat staring at her waiting for answers to his questions. "The Malibu has some scratches along the door of the driver side. I have no idea how they got there but I can't bear to look at my car like that for one more second. I called a few different places on yesterday to see if I could find a shop that would paint it before we go to Cancun." She lied. She rolled her eyes up in her head pretending to be annoyed. "That was the guy from Black Customs calling me to tell me they could do it." Xay pursed his lips giving her a look that let her know he wasn't falling for the bullshit that had just slipped from her lips. "What?"

"Do I look like I was born yesterday?" He asked but didn't give her a chance to reply. "*The Malibu has some scratches along the door of the driver side. I have no idea how they got there but I can't bear to look at my car like that for one more second.*" He mocked. "Really Kaliyah? All I am going to say is I hope that you know what you are doing."

"What are you talking about?" Kaliyah continued to play stupid but she knew that she was busted. She knew that he was on to her.

Xay sucked his teeth and smacked his lips. "So you are just going to keep playing dumb? You know good and damn well what I am talking about. Your little trifling ass done went and scratched that damn car up so that you would have an excuse to get close to that guy Thrill. You ain't slick!" he read her. "Ain't shit happen to your car until I told you about him owning that shop over on 117th St. Now, all of a sudden your car done got scratched up. Your car that you keep in the garage." He rolled his eyes again and waited to see what lies she would try to come with next.

Finally she'd given up trying to lie to her best friend, who she knew could see through her bullshit better than anyone else. "Fine Xay, I keyed the door of the car." She admitted laughing.

Xay shook his head and burst out laughing. "Bitch, you will do anything for a dollar!"

"Whatever!" Kaliyah laughed too because she knew that he was right. "I'm going to work my magic on his ass, clean his bank account and leave his ass high and dry before he even knows what hit him. He's probably never even had a woman who looked half as good as me pay him any attention. Just my conversation alone is going to cause him to throw money at me like I'm a stripper!"

"Girl..." Xay began but was interrupted by the ringing of his cell. *I love it when you call me big poppa*...the phone sang. Xay reached inside his bag and took out his phone. His glossed lips twisted into a smirk. He pressed send and answered. "Hello."

"Where are you?" The voice on the other end asked.

"I'm out with Kaliyah..."

"I want to see you." Xay could hear the lust in his voice and he knew exactly what time it was. "Is that possible?"

"Shouldn't you be at work?" Xay's blue eyes glanced at the time that was displayed on the clock on the dashboard and then briefly over at Kaliyah. She wasn't paying him any attention her eyes were on the road and her mind was on Thrill's bank account.

"I took the day off!" The voice on the other end snapped. "Now can I see you or not? It's simple, either yes or no."

"Yes, it's possible." Xay continued to play it cool.

"Good meet me at our normal spot. There'll be a key waiting for you at the front desk."

"Yeah...okay, I'll see you in a few." Xay pressed end and ended the call.

"Hmph, who are you going to see in a few?" Kaliyah asked before he could say anything.

"Child, who else but Cohen?" He lied easily. Kaliyah wasn't the only low-down scheming thirsty bitch in the car but he knew how to keep his shit to his self. He live by the phrase, never let your left hand know what your right is doing. He knew that sometimes it paid to keep your lips sealed. "Can you swing me by the crib so that I can get my car?"

"Sure can." She was kind of relieved that he had other plans. That way he wouldn't interfere with her plans for Thrill. She needed to be focused and he would only act as a distraction. She couldn't afford to have him messing up her money.

The rest of the drive was quiet. When they reached Xay's house, he excitedly hopped out of the car. "Pop the trunk so that I can get my bags." He instructed. Kaliyah reached down and pulled the latch that opened the trunk.

"I'll call you later." Xay promised before slamming the door and then going

back to the trunk to get his bags. After getting his things, he waved bye to

Kaliyah as she backed out of his driveway.

Chapter Eleven

Kaliyah strolled into Black Customs on a mission. She rolled her eyes behind her shades when she saw Jamal standing at the counter. She really didn't feel like dealing with him drooling all over her. She wasn't there to fraternize with the help. She was there to handle business with the boss!

She sashayed up to the counter and removed her shades. "Good afternoon, I'm here to see…" Her words trailed off as she noticed Thrill walking from the back towards the front. Today he had his dreads pulled back rocking a white beater and a pair of black workman's Dickies. He was chewing on a toothpick. He possessed the sexiest walk that Kaliyah had ever seen. As much as she wanted to deny it, she was extremely attracted to him. *Focus bitch! Focus!* She mentally chastised herself.

"You're here to see who, beautiful?" Jamal smiled looking her up and down. He gave her entire body the once over before returning his focus to her face. He licked his lips as he eyed her full pink glossed lips wondering how they'd taste. "What can I do for you?" He grinned like a Cheshire Cat. He noticed that something behind him had her attention and turned to see what it was. He saw Thrill making his way up to the counter. Just that quickly his envy of Thrill started to eat at him. Careful not to let it show, he turned his attention back to Kaliyah. He was determined to get her attention. He reached across the counter and touched the hand that she had resting on the counter. "What can I do for you beautiful?"

Kaliyah snatched her hand back and shot him a disgusted look. "Uh-uhh don't be touching me!" She snapped. A few guys that had witnessed the entire scene erupted in laughter.

"Damn!" Scooter teased continuing to laugh.

"My bad, baby...I didn't mean any harm." Jamal quickly apologized feeling slightly embarrassed by her reaction and the fellas' laughter. He hadn't expected her to react in that way. She'd treated him as if he were contagious. He looked over at the guys who were still laughing. Truth was he didn't find shit funny.

"Don't y'all have some work to do?" Thrill asked as he approached the counter. He didn't like a bunch of goofing off in his place of business because it made them look unprofessional in front of the customers. He also didn't like how they all lost it whenever an attractive woman walked in. *Lame ass niggas.* He thought to himself. He glanced at Jamal and wanted to smack him upside the head for acting so damn thirsty! "I see you made it." He acknowledged

Kaliyah who was standing in front of him wearing an agitated expression.

"Yeah, I did." She rolled her eyes at Jamal and then fixed her grey eyes on Thrill. "You need to teach your employees how to conduct themselves in a more respectable manner." She snapped.

"Excuse me?" Thrill asked. "What seems to be the problem?"

Jamal quickly spoke up before Kaliyah could say anything. He couldn't understand why she was making such a big deal out of something so small. "I touched her on her hand. Honestly, I didn't mean any harm. I was only being friendly." He explained feeling even more embarrassed now and wishing that a hole would miraculously open up in the floor so that he could go through it.

"That's not friendly, it's rude!" Kaliyah corrected him.

Thrill saw another customer walking in and tried to defuse the situation. "I apologize for his behavior and I will speak to him about it later, okay?"

"Yeah, okay."

"Jamal, can you take care of those customers right there?"

"Yeah boss...no problem." He was pissed and even though he was trying hard to conceal it. It still showed all over his face. He walked from behind the counter and went to greet the customers that had just walked in.

"Let's go outside so that I can take a look at your car." Thrill said to Kaliyah. She turned and took the lead and he followed her outside. Once they were outside he took a look at the scratches that were on the door of the car. "Who in the world did you piss off?" He laughed.

"What are you talking about?" Kaliyah asked confused.

He removed the toothpick from his mouth and continued to inspect the car looking to see if there were any more scratches before looking up at her. "Only a female would do something like this? Don't no niggas be going around keying people's cars. So who did you piss off? Were you messing with somebody's boyfriend?"

"No...I have no idea how this happened." She lied. "I was up at the mall shopping and when I came out...this is what I found." She pointed to the door of her car.

Thrill folded his arms across his chest. "Yeah, you pissed some chick off." Then a funny thought crossed his mind. "Or maybe it was dude that you were with at Escorpion's. He was pretty pissed when he left."

Though she really wanted to curse him out she bit her tongue and remembered why she was there. "Oh so you find how you ruined my date to be funny, huh?"

"Shawty, I didn't ruin shit." He corrected her. "You did. You were the one who couldn't keep your eyes off of me while you were supposed to be with him but we are not going to get into all of that. I can paint your car but the only thing is, I won't be able to start on it right away. Why didn't you tell me you were driving around in Barbie's dream car? I don't have this color pink. We will have to order it."

Kaliyah let out a sigh and ran her fingers over her hair like she was upset. "Shoot!"

"I'm sorry Shawty, I really am. I tried." Thrill apologized.

"It's okay. I guess, I will have to just wait to get it done when I come back from Cancun. I wanted it done before then but oh well..." she looked disappointed, playing her role to the fullest.

"When are you leaving for Cancun?"

"In three days."

"Can I go with you?"

"What?"

"I didn't say what. I asked if I could go." He flirted looking her in her eyes. Their eyes met briefly and then she quickly looked away. He found it cute how she kept trying to play like she wasn't interested.

"The point of me going to Cancun is to relax and get away from all things stressful for a few days." She replied and then looked up at him again. "Taking you would be defeating the purpose."

He laughed at her smart remark. "Really? Hmmm...I bet if you took me, you'd be singing a different tune before the trip was over. I'm not trying to brag but I've had quite a few women refer to me as the perfect stress reliever." He licked his lips.

Kaliyah felt the spot between her legs become moist and her clit start to throb. "Whatever."

"Your mouth is saying whatever but it looks like you think there may be some truth to what I just said." He looked down at her hardened nipples pressing against the thin fabric of the halter top that she was wearing and nodded. "At least your body does anyways."

"Can we please focus on my car?" She folded her arms over her chest, trying to hide her hardened nipples.

"Of course."

"So there is no way that you can order the paint and have it shipped here overnight?"

"I could but that will cost you more."

"Do I look like I am concerned with the cost?" She asked. "Whatever you need to do to have my car painted. Do it." She opened her bag, took out her wallet and pulled out Kent's credit card. "Can I pay now?"

"Oh shit look at you…ballin'!" Thrill teased. "Yes, you can pay now. Follow me inside to my office so that I can make a few calls to order the paint."

Inside Thrill's office Kaliyah sat in one of the chairs across from him on the other side of his desk. She listened as he talked to someone about having the paint that she needed for her car shipped overnight. He gave them all of the necessary information needed to ship it and then asked her for her credit card. She noticed the confused expression that covered his face as he read off the information that was on the card. When he was done, he hung up the phone and handed her the card. "You don't look like a Kent Moore to me. Who's that? Your sugar daddy?"

"As a matter of fact, it's my dad since you must know." She'd already had her answer ready because she had a feeling he might ask about the name on the card. "Can I go ahead and pay you for painting the car now too?"

"Yeah, if you want. We can do that when we walk back up front." He could see that she was a little more relaxed this time than she'd been the first few times that he'd seen her. He had a feeling he knew why. Now she knew that he had a little bread and her bougie ass was trying to see what she could get. He was very familiar with her type. He decided to use her gold-digging ways to his advantage because she had something that she wanted as well.

"So when are you going to stop playing games and let me take you out?"

Hmmm now we're talking. She'd known that he would try again to holla at her. "Why would I go anywhere with you after the way that you've treated me?"

He shook his head. "Shawty, I haven't treated you any way at all. You did that to yourself. You were a straight up bitch from the first moment that I laid eyes on you and tried to introduce myself to you because you felt that I was beneath you. You thought that I was some bum ass nigga with no job, out on the corners hustling. You judged a book by its cover without knowing anything about me so I had every right to carry shit with you the way that I did." He explained. "But I am trying now to move past that and allow the past to be the past. Regardless of how shit started out between us it doesn't have to continue that way. As a matter of fact we can start over right now." He stood up and straightened out his clothes and then extended his hand to her. "Hello Ms. Lady my name is Trever but everyone calls me Thrill."

Kaliyah just sat there staring at his hand for a few second before finally reaching out and shaking it. "I'm Kaliyah." She played along.

"It's nice to meet you, Kaliyah. I think that you are breathtakingly beautiful and I was wondering could I by any chance get your number so that I can call you some time. I'd love to take you out to dinner and show you a nice time if that is alright with you?" Out of habit he licked his lips.

Kaliyah didn't know which she wanted more, his lips sucking on her lips below or his money. She pretended to think about his question for a while. "Okay, I'll have dinner with you. I guess that will make up for how you ruined my last date." She stood from her seat ready to leave.

Thrill opened the door to his office for her and she walked out in front of him. "You didn't have any business with his whack ass anyways. You need a real nigga in yo life." He commented as he walked behind her watching how her ass switched in the little skirt that she was wearing.

Kaliyah didn't respond she just kept walking and smiling to herself. *Nah, I need your money in my life!*

Chapter Twelve

The next night Kaliyah found herself seated across from Thrill inside of The Oceanaire Seafood Room, one of the best seafood spots in Atlanta. It was one of her favorite spots. She'd been there quite a few times. Earlier that day, Thrill had called and asked her if he could take her out to dinner. He'd said that he wanted to see her before she left for her trip. She'd accepted thinking that getting in good with him before she left would get the ball rolling for when she came back. She knew that she needed to get on his good side if she planned on getting in his pockets.

She looked across the table at Thrill, who was looking like an edible God in a cream short sleeved Polo button up with brown Polo shorts and a pair of cream Polo shoes. Tonight he was wearing jewelry for the first time since she'd met him. On his right wrist was a diamond bracelet and on his left wrist was a Rolex. Kaliyah could tell by the way that the diamonds sparkled underneath the lighting that they were definitely real. She knew that he'd paid a pretty penny for it.

"How's your food?" Thrill asked when he looked up and noticed Kaliyah staring at him.

"Everything is delicious."

"I'm glad that you are enjoying it." He took the time to look at her really good. He was so glad that she'd chosen to not to wear a wig tonight. To him she looked much better without it.

"Why are you staring at me?" Kaliyah asked.

"I was just thinking to myself how beautiful you are without those wigs." He admitted truthfully. He saw the expression on her face change and quickly explained himself. "You're beautiful either way. It's just that your natural beauty is the best to me." She blushed. "So tell me about your family? Your mom, dad, sisters, brothers." Again he noticed her expression change.

"My mother's dead. I don't know my dad and I don't have any sisters or brothers."

Thrill looked at her confused. "Hold up, I thought that you used your dad's card to pay for the paint for your car and to have it painted."

Shit! She cursed herself for being so stupid. She'd forgotten all about the lie that she'd told him the day before. "I-I did but he's not my real dad. He just stepped in and took care of me. My real dad left before I was born." She picked at her food with her fork.

"Oh...sorry about your mother." He said sincerely.

"Don't be." Kaliyah replied dryly. "It wasn't your fault. She did it to herself."

He could see the pain in her eyes and felt sorry for her. He knew it had to be hard not having her mother. "If you don't mind me asking what happened to her?"

"Drugs...men...the streets." She'd been looking off into space but finally brought her eyes to meet his. "What about you? Where are your parents? Do you have sisters or brothers?"

"No sisters or brothers. My dad lives in VA but my mom is here in Atlanta and I have a twelve year old son." Kaliyah watched intensely as he spoke. She could see the love in his eyes as he spoke about his son and for some reason it started to make her emotional. He took his phone out and went to his pictures. "Here's a picture of my boy."

She leaned over and looked at the picture. "He's handsome."

"He get it from his pops." Thrill bragged smiling at her.

"Whatever." She rolled her eyes at him.

"Whatever." He repeated mockingly. "I see that you love that word because you say it a lot."

Kaliyah was about to speak when her phone rang. "Excuse me." She told Thrill before reaching inside of her clutch and taking out her phone. The word Restricted flashed on the screen. She looked at the screen puzzled and then pressed send to answer. "Hello." Whoever was on the other end didn't say anything but she could hear noises in the background. "Hello." She repeated. Whoever it was on the other end hung up.

Thrill saw the confused expression and asked. "Is everything alright?"

"Yeah, everything's fine." Her phone started to ring again, the word restricted was flashing on the screen again. She pressed send and answered. "Hello." She spoke into the phone annoyed. Again no one said anything. She turned her phone off completely and put it back in her bag. She didn't understand why someone had chosen to play on her phone but she wasn't about to allow it to ruin her night. To be honest she was really enjoying herself with Thrill. He wasn't so bad after all but she still kept in mind her purpose for being there in the first place.

The two of them continued to talk and get to know each other. After leaving the restaurant Thrill wanted to go and get some Krispy Kreme donuts. Kaliyah didn't mind at all. They would be her late night snack.

As they stood in line at the Krispy Kreme the two of them laughed and talked about different things. Someone from the outside looking in would've thought they were a couple.

"So have you thought anymore about me going with you to Cancun?" Thrill teased.

"Nope." Kaliyah laughed.

"Damn, why are you so mean? I thought that we were friends now and had finally buried the hatchet." Thrill pretended to be hurt.

"I wouldn't go so far as to say that we are friends. I mean, we're cool."

"I'll take that for now but trust me, you'll be singing a different tune soon."

"Whatever." She continued to laugh.

"*Whatever.*" Thrill mocked wrapping his arms around his from behind.

"Excuse you?" Kaliyah said but didn't bother moving or asking him to move. "What do you think you're doing?"

"It's called showing affection." He replied. "Mean as you are, I'm sure that you have no idea what that is but don't worry. I'll teach you."

"I do know what affection is, thank you. I just don't remember giving you permission to touch me." She still didn't bother trying to move.

Thrill chuckle. "Oh shit, I probably should move before you spazz out on me like you did Jamal."

Kaliyah rolled her eyes at the mention of Jamal's name. "Uggh…I do not like that guy. He gives me the creeps."

"Jamal is cool, Shawty. Stop being so uptight."

"Whatever."

When they reached her house, Thrill got out and walked her to her door. "I enjoyed myself tonight. Maybe we can do this again sometime soon." He told her.

"Yeah, I'd like that." She admitted feeling slightly disappointed that the night had come to an end. "Hey…ummm…would you like to come in for a drink?"

"I can." She turned and unlocked the door. She pushed the door open and went inside and he followed. He looked around at all of the expensive Italian leather furniture that adorned her living room. Her living room furniture was pink like her car. He felt like he had just walked into Barbie's house. Everything was pink and black.

"Let me guess your favorite color is pink?" He said walking further into the living room and looking at the horrible pink and black polka dotted curtains that hung from her window.

"Yes it is. Why do you have something against the color pink?" She asked tossing him a glance over her shoulder.

"To answer your question, no I don't have anything against the color pink. As a matter of fact one of my favorite things is pink." He winked at her.

She felt juices leak from her pussy and drench the seat of her panties. "Whatever. You are just nasty and full of slick comments aren't you?"

"I think that you like my slick comments." He said reaching over and caressing her cheek. His touch felt good against her skin, she didn't want to mess up her plan by jumping the gun and giving him the goodies but she was so turned on that she could barely focus. "Have a seat." She offered. He sat down on the loveseat. "Can you excuse me for a minute? I have to go and get out of this dress."

"I could help if you want." He suggested.

"No thank you. I believe that I can handle it all by myself." She assured him before heading upstairs.

Thrill got up and walked around the living room looking at the different pictures that hung on the walls and sat on the mantel over the fireplace. They were all pictures of Kaliyah and some of her and a white guy. He took one of the pictures down from the mantel. The frame said best friends in big pink letters. The guy in the picture along with Kaliyah looked familiar for some reason but Thrill couldn't put his finger on where he'd seen him or how he knew him.

"I see you have made yourself right at home." Kaliyah said as she was walking back into the room wearing a pair of shorts and a cami. Thrill placed the frame back where he'd gotten it from. "Come on let's go into the kitchen." He followed as she led the way. The kitchen wasn't much different from the living room. It too was decorated in pink and black.

Thrill took a seat at the island on one of the pink stools. "What is up with you and all of this pink? I mean, I get that it' your favorite color but damn."

"Why are you so bothered by my pink?" She place her hand on her hip.

Thrill laughed and bit his bottom lip eyeing her seductively. "I haven't seen your pink yet lil mama but I assume that any man would be bothered by it. In a good way." He winked.

"Get your mind out of the gutter." In an attempt to change the subject she asked, "It's a little chilly in here isn't it?"

Thrill wasn't about to let her off that easy. "I can make it real hot in here for you if you let me." He watched her reaction closely as she shifted her weight from one foot to the other nervously.

"No thank you." That is what her mouth said but her body was screaming...*Yes, please do!* "What would you like to drink?"

"Do you have any Patron?"

"Yes I do. Do you want the white or the red?"

"White."

"Coming right up." She started out of the kitchen to go into the dining room and fix their drinks.

"Hold up! Where are you going?" He asked curiously.

"Into the dining room where the mini bar is. What are you afraid to sit in here alone while I go and fix our drinks?" She asked sarcastically looking at him. Their eyes met and she had to look away. The sexual tension between the two of them was off the charts. She knew that when they finally got it in it was going to be explosive. She couldn't believe how attracted to him she'd become.

"I'm not afraid of anything. Just don't be in there putting no shit in my drink trying to drug me and take advantage of me."

"Trust me you don't have that to worry about with your cocky ass." She shot back.

"I'm not cocky baby just more confident than the niggas that you are used to fuckin with that's all."

Kaliyah turned and walked out of the kitchen switching her ass a lot more than she needed to. Thrill picked up on it but decided not to say anything. Instead of pouring the drinks she got two glasses and the bottle of Patron and brought all of it back into the kitchen. When she walked in Thrill had already eaten one of her donuts and was now on his second one.

"Damn, I suggest you go back to the car and get your box! I only offered you a drink not my entire box of donuts!" She snapped.

"Calm down Shawty." Thrill said smoothly, licking some of the glaze from his fingers. "This is just my second one but if it makes you feel any better you can have two of mine."

Kaliyah sucked her teeth and rolled her eyes. "I can't stand greedy people."

Thrill just laughed. He liked her little sassy attitude, it was cute. He still couldn't get over how much finer she was without the wig. He didn't even understand why she wore it. It took away from her natural beauty. She was a dime.

He hadn't even realized that he was staring until Kaliyah interrupted his thoughts by saying. "Excuse you but weren't you the same person who screwed up my date because you said that staring was rude?"

"My bad it's just that I can't get over how much better you look without that fake hair. I mean you are absolutely beautiful. Has anyone ever told you that you resemble Stacy Dash?"

Kaliyah blushed and ran her hands over her hair. "Yeah I get that a lot."

"She looks better but y'all favor." He had seen her head getting bigger and decided to mess with her.

She swatted him on the arm playfully. "Do you always have to be such an ass?"

He grabbed her hand and pulled her close to him. When she was close enough he covered her mouth with his and slipped his tongue between her lips. They kissed each other like they were two long lost lovers being reunited for the first time in years. Before Kaliyah knew it Thrill had pulled her cami over her head and thrown it on the floor and was devouring both of her nipples at one time.

Her eyes were closed as a moan escaped her lips. "Oh my goodness your mouth feels good! Please don't stop! It feels even better than I had imagined." When she realized what she had just said her eyes popped open.

Thrill just looked up at her and laughed as continued feasting on her thick nipples. He maneuvered one of his hands into her shorts and began to play in her wetness. He was surprised by just how wet she was. He inserted two of his fingers inside of her all the while using his thumb to stroke her clit. She was now holding onto him for dear life afraid that her legs might give out from what he was doing to her body. He let go of her nipples and took her mouth again. She kissed him like she was trying to drink all of him in and that was partially true. She gotten a taste of Thrill and it wasn't enough, she wanted more. He felt her muscles started to contract around his fingers and he knew that she was about to explode so he decided to take her over the edge.

"Go on and cum for me, Shawty." He whispered in her ear while nibbling and sucking on it. Then he went lower and nibbled and sucked on her neck.

"Oh shit! I'm cumming!" Kaliyah announced just as she lost control and a powerful orgasm took over her entire body. She couldn't remember ever cumming so hard in her life. She held on tight to Thrill as her body jerked violently. When her orgasm started to subside she opened her eyes to find Thrill watching her and wearing a cocky smirk. "What are you smirking about?"

He didn't reply he just leaned down and kissed her full lips again.

"That was the best orgasm I've ever had." Kaliyah admitted looking up at him while still trying to get herself together. Her legs felt like spaghetti strings. Thank goodness he was holding her up. "I have never had a man make me cum like that without even undressing me completely."

Thrill couldn't help but laugh. "You haven't seen nothing yet."

Chapter Thirteen

Two week later...

Kaliyah hadn't even been home for three hours and already she was on the phone dialing Thrill's number. She'd thought about him the entire time that she and Xay was in Cancun. So much that she hadn't really enjoyed herself. The man was like a drug, one taste and she'd become addicted. The phone rung several times before he answered.

"What's good lil mama?" He answered his voice like beautiful music to her ears.

"Hey, I was calling to check on my car." She lied trying to play things off. She didn't want to let on that she'd missed him. "I know that you are finished with it by now."

"Yeah, I'm done with it. You can come by and pick it up whenever you'd like."

A thought crossed her mind. "If you aren't busy after work. Could you drive it over to my house?" She asked. "I will drive you back home."

Thrill laughed. "Is that your way of getting me over to your place?"

She smiled. "Maybe."

"In that case, yeah I'll bring it to you when I get off." He looked up at the clock that was hanging on the wall over his desk. "I will be getting out of here in three more hours."

"Okay, I'll see you then." She hung up and went upstairs to run some water in the tub.

While the tub filled she began unpacking some of her things. She hummed her favorite song as she danced over to the closet and hung up some of the clothes that she'd bought. *Yeaaah (and all my ladies say)Yeaaah (the go go girls say)Yeaaah (hey hey)I got myself a sponsor Yeeaaah (to fill up a drank for me) Yeeaaah (to fill up a tank for me)Yeeaaah (to put something in the bank for)I got myself a sponsor.* Her phone sang. She took her time walking over to the phone. She'd talked to the one person that she wanted to talk to. She picked up the phone from her nightstand and looked at the screen. Kent's name was flashing on it. She really didn't feel like being bothered with him but she answered anyways. She wasn't no fool. Though she was feeling Thrill, she wasn't about to let any of Kent's paper slip through her fingers.

"Hello."

"Hello beautiful." Kent spoke into the phone. The sound of her sweet voice brought a smile to his lips. He'd missed her so bad while she was away. "How was your trip?"

"It was really nice." She told him as she walked over to the closet and continued to put her clothes away. "Thank you again. I really needed that."

"You're welcome, anything for you. You don't have to keep thanking me." He let her know. "Do you feel better?"

"Yes, I do."

"That's good. I have something for you."

She stopped what she was doing and flopped down on the bed, wondering what he had for her. He knew how much she loved receiving gifts. "Really?"

He giggled hearing the excitement in her voice. "Yes, really. Are you busy? I was thinking that you could meet me or I could bring it to you."

She was about to tell him she'd meet him when she remembered that

Thrill was coming over. "Ummm…how about I meet you tomorrow. I am kind of tired tonight. I was just about to take a bath and go to sleep."

A frown replaced the smile that he'd been wearing. "Gosh Kaliyah, I really wanted to see you. It's been nearly three weeks." He whined. "You're too tired to see me for just a little while?"

"Baby, I apologize but I am really beat. I promise that I will make it up to you tomorrow." When he didn't say anything she decided to try another route. "I'll allow you to lick the cream out of my cream pie." She promised referring to how she allowed him to lick his cum from her ass or pussy after he'd cum inside of her. She found it to be disgusting but he seemed to love it.

The mention of it made his dick swell. "You think you know how to get me don't you?"

She giggled. "I do."

"Okay baby, I guess I'll have to just wait until tomorrow to see you then."

"I apologize again baby but I am really tired."

"I understand. Go ahead and get some rest beautiful and I'll talk to you tomorrow."

"Okay...good night."

"Good night." They hung up. "Shit!" Kent cursed picking up his phone to call his plan B.

Kaliyah heard the phone ringing again as she made her way to the bathroom to check the water in the tub. She knew that the tub was full by now and prayed that it hadn't run over in the floor. She kept walking. She went into the bathroom and saw that the water at the top of the tub. She turned off the water and let some out before undressing and stepping inside the tub. She took her time and soaked before taking her bath and getting out. She dried off and slipped into a pair of pink shorts and a white Cami.

Thrill stood on Kaliyah's porch and rang the doorbell. He heard her unlocking the door and then she swung it open. "Hello, come in." She smiled stepping back out of the way.

"Hello to you, Ms. Lady." He replied noticing the big smile she was wearing. He walked inside and she closed the door behind him and locked it. He leaned over and kissed her on her cheek. "How was your trip?"

"It was nice." She replied feeling some kind of way by the peck on the cheek that he'd just given her.

He took a seat on the sofa and she sat down the other end. "It was nice? Just nice? See you should've let me go. Then you would've been turning flips bragging to the world about how great your trip to Cancun was." He winked.

"If you say so."

"I do." He confirmed. "Why are you sitting so far away?" he asked noticing the distance between them. "Before you left you were all over me. You come back and you are acting like you're afraid to sit close to a nigga."

"Oh, I'm acting differently but before I left your tongue was all down my throat. Now you're pecking me on the cheek like I'm your sister." She countered.

He laughed. "Woman stop being so damn difficult and bring your sexy ass here." She got up slowly pretending like she didn't want to go to him. Truly she wanted to dive in his arms. She sat down next to him. "Uh-uhh sit right here." He patted his lap. She got up and sat on his lap. He put his hand on the back of her head pulling her face to his and kissed her nice and slowly. She couldn't stop the moan that escaped her throat. She'd been thinking about his kisses for two weeks. She kissed him with so much passion that it was evident how much she'd missed him. He reached up and caressed her breasts.

"Mmmm…" She moaned his touch was hypnotizing. "I have been thinking about how hard you made me cum before I left. No man has ever made me cum like that?"

"Hmmm is that so?" He asked. "Like I told you before you have been fucking with the wrong niggas."

"Maybe but I don't want to talk about that right now." She kissed him on his lips. "I hope that you are not done. I've seen what you can do with your hands now I want to see what you can do with your dick." She stated matter-of-factly. She saw no need to sugarcoat shit. They were both adults.

"What would you think of me if I gave it up on the first night? What kind of man do you take me to be?" He teased.

"I don't know about all of that but I can tell you what I will think of you if you just tease me and not finish the job." She sucked on his bottom lip. "I will think that you are the kind of man who isn't capable of handling his business. You wouldn't want me to think that now would you?"

He could tell that she wanted him bad even badder than he wanted her and he wanted her bad. "Oh baby I am very capable of handling my business and I guarantee you that once I give you this dick you will say the same thing too after you wake up because when I am done with you all you will be able to do is roll over and go to sleep. My dick game is so good I will have you wanting to kill a bitch if you even suspect that she is looking my way." He boasted.

"How about you stop talking about it and show me because talk is cheap!"

She didn't have to say anymore. Thrill picked her up and she wrapped her legs around his waist. "Where is your bedroom?" He asked.

She told him the way to her bedroom. Once they were in her room, he laid her in the middle of the bed and removed her shorts. As he undressed his eyes swept over her beautiful body and they loved what they saw. She was absolutely breathtaking. He removed everything except for his boxers, which he saved for last. Kaliyah laid back propped up on her elbows waiting for him to discard them so that she could see what he was working with. She could already see a huge tent in them but she needed to see the real thing to be sure that her eyes were not playing tricks on her.

"Are you sure that this is what you want?" He continued to tease her.

"Boy if you don't stop playing with me!" She warned growing impatient like a child waiting to open up their gift on Christmas morning.

Thrill pulled down his boxers and let them fall to the floor before stepping out of them. His nine inches stood at full attention pointing at her as if to say "All of this is for you." It wasn't just long as hell but it was also thick as hell too.

Kaliyah's mouth fell open as she looked at the size of Thrill's dick. She began to wonder if her kitty kat could take all of him. She wasn't sure but she was damn sure going to try. "Damn!" Was the only word that came to mind.

Thrill reached down and took a Magnum out of his pants pocket and tore it open before sliding it on. Then he crawled onto the bed between Kaliyah's thighs. He felt her legs trembling as he position himself between them. "Relax I got you, lil mama. I promise that I'll be gentle."

"I'm…good." She said nervously and very unconvincingly.

He kissed her passionately and began playing with her nipple in hopes of relaxing her some. Soon she was moaning and begging him to put it in she had forgotten all about her nervousness. He put the head of it to her opening and eased in slowly. With her being so wet it did make the entry a lot easier but it was still a little bit of a struggle. You would think that since she went through more dicks than underwear in a week she could take Thrill with no problem but that wasn't the case.

"Oh shit!" She screamed when she felt the head slide in. She unwrapped her arms from around his neck and tried to back away from under him but he held her in place and eased more of himself inside. "Oh my goodness. You are ripping my pussy open!" She screamed.

He just kissed her to muffle her screams and then in one shift motion he pushed himself in as far as he could go. Kaliyah was going crazy because she hadn't imagined that it would hurt so much. He moved in and out at a slow and steady pace while continuing to kiss on her lips, ears, neck and breasts. After a while the pain started to subside and was replaced by pleasure. Thrill was hitting spots that she hadn't known existed. The dick got so good that she started trying to pull her own hair but it was too short for her to grip. He flipped her over and entered her from behind, still taking it easy not wanting to hurt her. He couldn't beat it up like he wanted to but it was okay because she had that good-good and it didn't matter to him how he was getting it just as long as he was getting it. He'd assumed that she might have some good pussy but he could've never imagined that it would be as good as it was. He was having a hard time trying not to bust too soon because she had the wettest warmest tightest pussy that he'd ever been in. That was due to all of the Kegel exercises that she did daily to keep her walls tight.

As he hit it from the back he bit her on her back and shoulders which turned her on even more. So much so that she started to throw the pussy back at him with no regards for the fact that she would probably be almost crippled by the time they were done.

"Oh shit baby throw that shit back at me girl." Thrill moaned as he gripped her hips and thrust inside of her like a madman. He assumed that it was okay for him to hit it like he wanted to since she was throwing it at him like she it didn't hurt anymore. All that could be heard throughout the entire room was the slapping of their skin up against one another, moaning and panting. The way they were sexing at this point was outright animalistic. Thrill pushed Kaliyah's head down onto the bed so that her ass was left up in the air and then he went into a zone tearing her pussy out the frame. He was in so deep that she could feel it in her stomach. He was fucking her so good that she thought that she might pass out from experiencing so much pleasure.

Thrill felt his nut building and he knew that he wasn't going to be able to hold out much longer. He reached around her and began playing with her clit without missing a beat. Kaliyah felt herself about to explode for the second time, unable to fight it she let go. Thrill pulled out and snatched the condom off and shot his load all over her ass.

"Fuck!" He roared collapsing next to her on the bed.

Chapter Fourteen

Kent sat at the table the next morning enjoying his morning coffee and reading the morning paper. He couldn't really concentrate on the article that he was reading. His mind was consumed with thoughts of Kaliyah. He couldn't wait to see her and kiss her sweet lips. A smile played on his lips as he thought about her. He'd missed her so much that he felt like they should do something special together. He thought hard about what they could do. He wanted to take her somewhere really nice and romantic. As he sat there thinking, his wife Jessica strolled into the kitchen.

"The boys and I are going out of town this weekend." She spoke interrupting his thoughts.

"Come again." He told her blinking in an effort to blink away his thoughts of Kaliyah.

Jessica placed her hand on her hip and turned to face her husband. "I said that they boys and I are going out of town this weekend." She hated him so much that it annoyed her to have to open her mouth to speak to him. If they could exist in the same house without looking at or talking to one another she would've been a very happy woman. She knew all about the little black bitch that he had on the side. She'd known since the beginning of their affair. She just didn't care enough to say anything. The little whore could have him as far as she was concerned. She was waiting for the boys to get grown so that she could pack her things and leave.

"That's fine." He didn't understand why she was telling him. She could leave and never return, it wouldn't have made a bit of difference to him. He got up from the table and pushed his chair in. "I'll see you tonight."

"Yeah." Jessica rolled her eyes and took a sip of the fresh cup of coffee that she'd just poured for herself.

Outside Kent got in his car and started the ignition. He opened his glove box and took out the little black box that held the diamond necklace that he'd bought for Kaliyah. He opened it and peeked inside before closing it back up and laying it in the passenger seat. "I can't wait to see the look on her face once she sees this." He said aloud putting the car in reverse and backing out of the driveway.

He'd decided to stop by and give Kaliyah the necklace on his way to work. He turned up the radio and hummed along to the song that played. All the way to her house he kept thinking of how happy she was going to be once she saw the gift that he had for her.

He turned onto her street and slowed in front of her driveway. He was about to turn in the driveway but what he saw caused him to stop. Kaliyah was standing in the doorway with her arms around a man. Kent wasn't sure if he was more upset at the fact that she was with another man or at the fact that he was a black man. She'd sworn to him on numerous occasions that she didn't date black men. She might didn't date them but she sure as hell fucked them. It didn't take a rocket scientist to figure out that the man had spent the night. She was still in her robe!

Kent felt his anger boiling over as he thought about how she'd had the nerve to lie to him the night before about being too tired to see him. She'd lied to him to be with whoever this man was, after he'd just paid for her to go to Cancun! He pressed the accelerater and sped off! "Ungrateful bitch!" He spat. He was hurt by untruthfulness but it was okay because she would be hurt too. Nobody fucked over Kent Moore and got away with it!

****

Xay pulled into the parking lot of Troutman & Saunders. He parked his cherry red Impala next to a burgundy BMW. Before getting out of the car he freshened up his lip gloss and popped in a mint. He grabbed his Dolce and Gabbana handbag and strutted towards the entrance of the building. Inside he took the elevator up to the second floor. When he stepped off the elevator he walked up to the receptionist's desk.

"Good afternoon. I'm here to see Kent Moore." He informed the white haired elderly woman.

"Good afternoon." She smiled politely looking up at Xay. "What is your name sir?"

"Xavier Baldwin."

"Okay, have a seat and I will let Mr. Moore know that you are here." She told him.

Xay took a seat in the waiting area and began thumbing through the pages of a fashion magazine. A few minutes later, the receptionist called from behind her desk. "Mr. Baldwin."

Xay looked up from his magazine and saw that the receptionist was standing. She waved him over. He placed the magazine back on the table where he'd gotten it from and walked over to her. "Yes ma'am."

"Mr. Moore will see you now." She informed him. "Follow me right this way."

She took the lead and Xay followed behind her, eyeing all of the expensive art that adorn the walls of the hallway. This was his first visit to Kent's office. Normally when they'd meet it would be somewhere more private, like a hotel but earlier when they'd spoken Kent had asked him to come by his office because he had something very important that he wanted to talk to him about. Ever since then Xay had been wrecking his brain trying his best to figure out what could possibly be so important that he'd invited him to his office. He was kind of nervous, as he wondered if he'd invited him here to break things off between them. They'd been having a secret affair for the past four months. An affair that had been very beneficial to Xay and he wasn't ready for it to end. He assumed that Kent had probably invited him to his office because he knew how out of control his temper could get and thought that he had a better chance of breaking things off with him here with there being less confusion than if he did it somewhere private. *Hmph, if that's what his plan is then he'd better think again because I don't give a fuck where we are! If he thinks that he is about to end things between us and I am not going to show my tiny white ass up in here, he is dead wrong! There is no way in hell I*

am going to just tuck my tail between my legs and leave quietly and allow

Kaliyah to continue to live high off the hog while I get nothing! I will expose all

of his dirty little secrets! I will tell his white and all of his high and mighty friends

how much he loves dick! Xay thought to himself wearing a smirk.

They reached Kent's office and the receptionist tapped lightly.

"Come in." He heard Kent call from the other side.

The receptionist turned the knob and pushed the door open gently. "Yes sir, Mr. Baldwin."

Kent looked up from behind his desk. "Thank you, Mrs. Luther." She stepped out of the way and Xay walked in past her. She closed the door and left the two of them alone.

Xay took a seat in one of the brown leather chairs in front of Kent's desk and laid his handbag in the other one. "So what was so important that I needed to come down here to see you?" He got straight to the point.

"Well, hello to you too." He replied as he leaned back in his seat and unbuttoned his suit jacket to get more comfortable.

Xay rolled his eyes becoming impatient. "Look cut the bullshit. We've spoken to each other today. So what do you want?" He decided to warn Kent before he said something that set him off. "And please don't come out of your mouth and say some ol' dumb shit that is going to piss me off because I will set it off up in here honey!"

Kent set back up. "You will sit your ass in that seat and shut the hell up, is what you will do. Don't come strutting up in here like you run something. I am the one running the show, not you." He looked Xay directly in his eyes letting him know that he meant business. "Are we clear?" Xay rolled his eyes but didn't respond. "Let's not forget who makes it possible for you to live in that nice condo and live this luxurious lifestyle. It sure as hell isn't that little boyfriend of yours or that little part-time job you work at!" Xay still didn't utter a word. Satisfied Kent continued. "Now I called you here because I wanted to speak with you about Kaliyah."

Xay rolled his eyes up in his head and sucked his teeth. "You called me all the way down here to talk about Kaliyah?"

"Yes, I called you all the way down here to talk about Kaliyah!" Kent said through clenched teeth. He'd had just about enough of Xay's attitude and he wasn't about to tolerate much more. Xay had no idea just how powerful the man sitting in front of him was. He had connections with people who would get rid of Xay with no hesitation. It was only a matter of picking up the phone. "I have a few questions to ask you and I want the truth! I am not in the mood for any games right now."

"I'm listening." Xay replied. He was upset that Kent had called him there to talk about Kaliyah. True enough he'd known his position when he'd first gotten involved with Kent but the more time that passed he was getting tired of him always acting like Kaliyah was better than him. Obviously she wasn't because if she was all of that he wouldn't be in the picture. Also if she meant so much to him then she would know all of the low-down secrets that he knew about him.

"What do you know about this black guy that Kaliyah is screwing?"

Xay couldn't suppress his laughter. "Are you kidding me? Honey child, you have got to be kidding me! You called me all the way down here to ask me about who Kaliyah is fucking?"

"Do I look like I am fucking laughing?" Kent tried not to raise his voice. "I am serious!"

Xay jumped to his feet. "If you want to know anything about her pussy you go and ask her!" he snapped feeling some kind of way about how Kent

was trying to use him to spy on Kaliyah. Everything was always about her!

"Call me all the way down here for this bullshit! I could've been somewhere

else doing something else with my damn time!" He grabbed his bag and put it

on his shoulder. "Call me when…"

Kent jumped to his feet and slapped Xay so hard that his bag dropped

from his shoulder! "I said that I wasn't in the mood!" He said through clenched

teeth. Xay stood frozen in place unable to believe what had just happened. He

rubbed the spot where Kent had just slapped him. Kent walked around his

desk and stood next to Xay. "Now I am going to ask you again. What do you

know about this black guy that Kaliyah is screwing?"

"All I know is that he owns a customizing shop over on 117th St."

"How long has she been seeing him?"

"Not long…just a few weeks."

"What's his name?"

"Thrill is all I know."

Kent shook his head. What in the hell did Kaliyah see in someone with a name like that? "Has she said anything about having feelings for him?"

"No, not to me. You know how she is. It's all about the money with her."

"Money?" Kent repeated in disbelief. "I give her any and everything that she wants so it can't be about the money!"

Xay was still playing over in his head what had just happened. He really couldn't believe that Kent had the audacity to put his hands on him. Even though he knew there was a good chance of it happening again once he spoke his mind, that didn't stop him. "You know, I am confused as to why it matters so much to you who she's fucking. I mean, the truth of the matter is you are married and you are fucking me! She knows about your wife but she has no idea about me. How can you be upset by anything that she does?"

"Because I love her. I don't love you and I don't love my wife! Does that answer your question?" Kent roared. He was so upset about Kaliyah and Thrill that he was finding it difficult to control his anger. "You can leave now."

Xay picked up his bag and made his way towards the door. All sorts of thoughts were running through his head. Kent had made a big mistake by putting his hands on him. When he reached his car, he looked at his face in the mirror. The spot where Kent had slapped him was red. "That's alright. I've got

something for your ass Mr. Moore." He said aloud as he started up his car and
backed out of the parking lot.

THANK YOU'S

First and foremost I would like to thank God for everything. Without him nothing would be possible. I thank him for blessing me with this wonderful gift to be able to write and entertain people with my stories. Secondly, I would like to thank my three beautiful babies, Ny'Ajah, Camari, and AnTeyvion. You three are the reason that I grind so hard and continue to strive for more and to become a better me. I would like to thank my mom, Angela Taylor and my dad, Paul Hill. I am thankful for and appreciate you both. To my grandmothers Ann West and Mable Hill, I love you both and thank you for being there for me whenever I have needed you both. To my sister and my best friend Tinika Taylor, I love you more than life itself. You are my rock, the one person I can depend on when everyone else in this harsh world has turned their backs on me! I treasure every moment that the two of us spend together.

To all of my aunts, uncles and cousins, I love you guys. R.I.P to my uncles Steve and Calvin, I miss you both very much. A special shout out to my uncle Al Kelly, even though we don't get to see each other much anymore because of our hectic schedules, I love you to pieces and thank you so much for the love and support that you have shown me. Thank you to my sister from another mother Denise Mason, I love you girl and appreciate you. Thanks for listening to my constant drama lol even though I already know what you be saying in your head when I be yapping…lmao! To my cousin, Teresa Porter (my late night, early morning riding partner). Thanks for being there for me the times when I have needed you the most to just be a listening ear.

Now I'd like to thank all of the fans who have followed my work! Thank you to each and every one of you who has ever purchased any of my work or just taken time to read an excerpt of mine. I appreciate it. Thank you to Cash who has believed in a sista since day one. I can't begin to express to you how much your friendship and constant advice and support means to me, I love you and will always treasure our friendship.

To all of the wonderful authors who have supported me or just given me advice, thank you. Aaron Bebo, Jason Hooper, Aleta Williams, Authoress Redd, Andrionna Williams, Candice Stevenson. There are a few of you who have been some real riders so I definitely have to shout you out. Kendra Littleton, Brandi McClinton, Novie Cuteyez, Sharon Blount, Skeet the Poet, Karen Patterson, Chyna Blue, Raychelle Williams, Shayna Williams, Judy Richburg, and Shaniqua Townes. Shout to one of the best book clubs BRAB! You guys rock!!! Thank you all so much. If I have forgotten any one I truly apologize. I suck at this lol. Please know that it wasn't intentional.

CPSIA information can be obtained at www.ICGtesting.com
Printed in the USA
LVOW05s1450191213

366067LV00023B/1182/P